Also available in **DEFᵢNᵢTᵢONS**

Visit the Random House Children's Books
website at www.**kids**at**randomhouse**.co.uk for a
full list of Definitions titles and other great reads.

HAP PY
by Keith Gray

RED FOX DEFINITIONS

HAPPY

A RED FOX BOOK : 0099439522

First published in Great Britain by Mammoth,
an imprint of Egmont Children's Books Limited

Mammoth edition published 1998
Red Fox edition published 2002

1 3 5 7 9 10 8 6 4 2

Set in Adobe Garamond
Red Fox Books are published by Random House Children's Books,
61-63 Uxbridge Road, London W5 5SA,
a division of The Random House Group Ltd,
in Australia by Random House Australia (Pty) Ltd,
20 Alfred Street, Milsons Point, Sydney, NSW 2061, Australia,
in New Zealand by Random House New Zealand Ltd,
18 Poland Road, Glenfield, Auckland 10, New Zealand,
and in South Africa by Random House (Pty) Ltd,
Endulini, 5A Jubilee Road, Parktown 2193, South Africa

THE RANDOM HOUSE GROUP Limited Reg. No. 954009

A CIP catalogue record for this book is available from the British Library.

Printed and bound in Great Britain by Bookmarque Ltd, Croydon, Surrey

For Hannah,
because she's great!

With thanks to
Steve Brown for letting me steal some of his best lyrics;
Steve Coxon, Ian Elliot, Dave Gelder, Ade and Rob Moody,
Jim Taylor, Simon Welton amd Dave Worley for helping me
nurture my own, admittedly dubious, musical talents;
and Carolyn and Miriam for their infinite patience.

Press *play*. And turn it up LOUD!

Part One

Will

THE OTHER BAND

BAN EASY LISTENING!
SHOOT CLIFF! LIVE TONIGHT!

The scrawled, black and white posters were pinned to every tree and lamppost along Mosley Street. Even the bus stop and the two back-to-back telephone kiosks on the corner hadn't escaped. A red Nissan Micra parked at the side of the road had three plastered across the windscreen and another one slap-bang in the middle of its bonnet. I thought it was more than the little car deserved.

Danny peeled one off a telegraph pole. 'Is that what they're called?' he asked. '*Shoot Cliff*?'

I nodded.

He handed me the poster. 'Very witty,' he said sarcastically.

I looked at it only briefly; it was tacky and amateurish. Our posters would be better. I scrunched it up and tossed it into the gutter.

We'd been able to hear the band from at least two streets away; what they lacked in ability they seemed determined to make up for in volume. We crossed the road and headed towards the scout hut as the shrieking of a heavily distorted guitar cut through the evening air. An elderly lady walking her rat-like little dog shook her head at us and mumbled, 'Shouldn't be allowed,' as she passed by. The small, leaning scout hut didn't look fit to withstand such an onslaught for long. The drums thundered and boomed, and for a moment I thought I saw the old roof rattle. Above it all the singer howled.

'Must be in pain,' Danny said.

'He's probably got a headache,' I told him.

He laughed, then said, 'I really don't think we're gonna find anyone here. I mean, seriously!' He pulled a face at the noise coming from the scout hut.

'It's worth a try,' I said. 'They're the only other band around here.'

He shrugged, but followed me as I hopped over the short, metal-worked fence and headed across the gravel driveway. I have to admit that I was doubtful too. There was only a hire van and a couple of mountain bikes parked beside the hut, which didn't bode at all well for audience figures. The main thought running through my mind, however, was that if this was the only other band in Cleeston, then people must be gagging for some decent music around here. And we'd be worshipped like the Gallagher brothers.

We had to pay to get in. A man with fading ginger hair was sitting behind a table in the cloakroom, and he pointed to a sign in front of him which had a huge '£3.50' written on it in felt-tip. Danny was outraged. He tried to argue, but couldn't make himself heard above the music as it clamoured around him, and in the end I had to fork out for both of us. The man watched me carefully, putting an instantly suspicious eye on me. I just stared back at him. It's nothing new, everybody does it. Either that or they ask me what the weather's like up here.

We hadn't been inside the scout hut for years, but they still had the same cracked and faded linoleum covering the floorboards, and the walls still needed a fresh coat of paint. Nothing much had changed, it just seemed smaller. I followed Danny through into the main room where we had spent most of our Tuesday nights as kids playing Jacob's Ladder and learning how best to make 'woggle' sound like a rude word, and was completely shocked by the size of the audience.

The people were packed tightly all the way up to the back wall forcing Danny and me to fight with our elbows to find space. Or so it seemed. The song ended with a crash of cymbals and there was a smattering of applause from the kids around us, but from down at the front there were great whoops of appreciation and calls for more.

'That's where we should be,' I said, peering over the tops of the heads, trying to work out how many people were here.

Danny didn't look too sure.

'Down at the front,' I said. 'I want to see how well they play.'

'Can't you tell just by listening?' Danny asked, then reluctantly followed me as I pushed my way through the crowd.

What had originally appeared to be a packed house soon proved to be well over half-empty. The audience dropped from what had first looked to be at least a hundred, to only just scraping thirty. They were all in fact crammed against the back wall, and there was a group of only five or six lads down at the front with acres of space all to themselves. They wore Shoot Cliff T-shirts (a picture of a red double-decker bus riddled with bullet holes) and ripped jeans. As the next song kicked in they flung themselves around, leaping up and down, barging into one another, windmilling their arms, banging their heads, almost in time to the music. And I quickly realised that the rest of the audience was in fact only trying to give them room for their manic dancing.

I looked at Danny, who shook his head. He tugged on my arm, making it clear he wanted to leave, pulling a face. But I ignored him. He was beginning to get on my nerves. Here I was, trying to make his dreams come true, offering him the chance of a lifetime, and all he could do was pull faces and want to go home early.

'You don't like this, do you?' he shouted in my ear.

I shook my head.

'This is terrible,' he told me above the din.

I nodded.

'Come on, then. Let's go.' And when I didn't move he tried a different tack. 'I thought you said you were meeting Beth.'

'Not till later,' I told him. I grabbed his wrist and pointed at the figure eight on his watch, then gave him a look which quite clearly meant *shut up*. I was determined to get my three pounds fifty pence worth. At least the dancers were kind of entertaining.

The band were a five piece – two lead guitars, one bass, a drummer and a singer. They billed themselves as a 'hardcore fusion between punk and heavy metal', which I guess accounted for the terrible haircuts. The lank and greasy mullets sported by the two lead guitarists were laughable, but the singer's multi-coloured buzz cut was downright scary – red and blue and green and purple and pink. He was wearing a pair of checked trousers which had been ripped just below the knees to make shorts, and a huge pair of Doc Martens. He was naked and sweaty from the waist up. I couldn't believe how willing some people were to get up on stage in full view of everyone only to make fools of themselves. But I guessed you could see it on *Top of the Pops* virtually every week of the year.

I don't just like music, I love it. It matters to me. (When I watch the adverts on TV I can name nine out of ten of the tunes they play in the background.) I'm proud to boast one of the comp's largest CD collections, if not *the* largest, and

I'm sure it's going to be worth quite a bit of money one day. I'm not narrow-minded in my taste, and like to think of myself as open to stuff I wouldn't necessarily put in my player. I'll give anything a try at least once . . . But this was awful. I wondered briefly what Lord Baden-Powell would make of it if he were here, as the music screamed on at something like ninety miles per hour, with squealing tyres, a pack of tomcats fighting to get out on the back seat, and a madman at the wheel.

'Dib dib die! Dob dob death!' the singer howled, throwing himself around on the makeshift stage.

They had no class, no style, and less talent. But I still found it uplifting to watch them. Mainly because I knew I could do better. Much, *much* better. The noise they made was so harsh it squeezed the sides of my skull. My head ached for a melody. I'm not a fan of Cliff Richard, but I felt it was these guys who really needed shooting.

I would have left then; Danny was bored, in a world of his own, and even the mad dancers down the front were losing their appeal. But when the song finished the singer wandered off to the side, grabbing a can of Coke and wiping a towel across his sweaty chest. The guitarists sat themselves down at the other side, and the stage was left free for the drummer. He was a stocky, ginger-haired kid I recognised from the comp; Gary or Gareth or something. I'd seen him around quite a bit, but had never shared any lessons with him. He was also naked from the waist up, but he was twice as broad as the singer, the skin stretched across his chest as tightly as on any of his drums. The mad dancers were all clapping and shouting, 'Come on, Gav! Ga-vin! Ga-vin!' making him grin in a shy, almost embarrassed kind of way. He counted himself in with his sticks, then proceeded to play one of the best drum solos I've ever heard.

I was stunned. It was incredible. It was as though he'd been trapped playing all those god-awful songs with the rest of the band, but now he was free. He used every single drum and cymbal in his kit, flying across them, getting faster and faster, louder and louder, never missing a beat. I suddenly realised the real reason why anybody paid hard-earned cash to see this band. I looked at Danny, and his mouth was hanging open. I knew how he felt; this guy was amazing. Incredible. I couldn't figure out what on earth he was doing hanging around with this bunch of losers, and immediately knew I could make him a better offer. He was loving it too, you could see it in his face, riding the sound around his drums and the bursting explosion of his cymbals, crashing, splashing, contorting his face as though his sticks were too hot to touch . . .

It was just a pity the police had to come and put a stop to his fun.

I didn't see them at first. Danny grabbed my arm and yanked me to one side as the two coppers strode down the middle of the room. The ginger-haired man who'd been collecting money on the door followed close behind them, looking worried. The drummer, Gavin, hadn't seen them either. They shouted at him to stop, but he was quite happy bashing merry hell out of his kit. The first policeman, the taller one, had to actually grab his sticks before he even realised they were there. Then he almost fell off his stool in surprise, and blushed a deeper red than his close-cropped hair.

'That's better,' the copper smiled. 'Peace at last, eh?'

The singer was already on his feet. 'Hey! What d'you think you're doing? We're in the middle of a gig!' He tried to stand in between the coppers and the stage. 'You can't do that! We're playing a gig!' And then the guitarists were shouting too. They crowded around the policemen, angry and indignant. 'What d'you think you're doing? That's not fair! You can't do that!'

Some of the audience disappeared at this point, not wanting to be involved with anything concerning the police. But most stayed on, probably thinking it could all turn out to be worth three pounds fifty after all.

The shorter policeman put a restraining hand on the singer's bare chest, but he violently shoved it away, still shouting.

The copper glared at him. 'Simmer down, laddy.' He looked at the rest of them. 'All of you. Just take it easy.' He glowered, waiting for the shouting to subside. He turned around slowly, staring at each of them until they calmed down enough to let him speak. He tilted his policeman's cap back a little on his head. 'Now listen,' he said when eventually everybody was quiet. 'We've had complaints about the noise.' He was turning on the spot, speaking to them all individually. 'And we've got to ask you to turn your volume down a little . . .' But he got no further than that. The band all burst out shouting angrily again, and the mad dancers suddenly joined in too. Even the man from the door was trying to make himself heard.

The singer was especially heated. He was easily as tall as the policeman and leaned in close to him, right into his face, fists clenched. But the copper stood his ground, even though he was surrounded and everybody was bellowing. His taller partner waded in to try and quiet everyone down again, but only ended up adding to the commotion. Nobody could hear anybody else's shouts above their own. There was a bit of pushing going on, and the pack of people staggered back and forth. The only person not shouting was the drummer. He was sitting behind it all looking quite confused, not sure what to do, and I suddenly felt sorry for him. Gigs just weren't meant to end like this. There hadn't been much applause so far.

And things seemed to go from bad to worse. The group of mad dancers started chanting, 'Shoot! Cliff! Shoot! Cliff!' picking up in volume. The tall copper looked exasperated, the shorter one furious. The band joined in the chant, punching the air. The man from the door waved his hands, trying to calm them down, but looking almost as though he were goading them on. The taller policeman tried to speak into the radio clipped to his uniform. The singer was stabbing a finger in the shorter one's chest. He was shouting, 'Shoot! Pig! Shoot! Pig!' The copper was red-faced with anger, warning the kid not to push it too far.

But he did.

He shoved the policeman hard with both hands, catching him by surprise, knocking him off balance, and almost in slow motion the policeman tumbled backwards into the drum kit. He crashed into the cymbals, knocked Gavin from his stool, and put his boot through the bass drum with an echoing boom.

Apart from the fading splash of a cymbal as it rolled across the wooden floor, the old scout hut was silent. The mad dancers and the guitarists all looked as though they were pretending to be invisible. The policeman picked himself up from the mess of tumbled drums. He had a face like thunder.

He retrieved his cap from the floor and put it back on, low over his eyes. He straightened his dark uniform slowly and carefully. He pointed at the singer. 'You. Outside.'

The singer didn't move. His technicoloured head bristled.

The copper stepped up to him. 'How much trouble do you want, sonny?' He was almost whispering, but everyone could hear him as plain as day. He looked as though he wanted to use his truncheon *really* badly. 'Outside!'

But still the singer held on, balefully staring the policeman in the eye for two or three long seconds. Only when it looked like the copper was going to be forced into saying something more did he move, pushing angrily through the audience who had crowded further forward now than at any other time during the gig. They quickly shrank back again when the policeman followed.

The taller copper surveyed the rest of us. He clapped his hands briskly, rubbing his palms together. 'Right. Show's over.' He smiled tightly at his little joke. 'You've got ten minutes to clear your gear, then I want you out.' He hooked a thumb over his shoulder to show them the way.

The guitarists groaned, but they didn't dare argue now – although they did need telling twice before any of them made a move. Surprisingly, it was the balding, ginger-haired man from the door who tried to reason with the policeman. I realised he must be the drummer's dad.

'Have a heart, chief. You don't need to clear them out, do you? Surely they can just turn the volume down a touch?' He smiled his best smile, and looked exactly like his son had done when the mad dancers had been chanting his name. 'Come on, they might be famous one day.'

The policeman wasn't convinced. 'Not without a singer they won't.'

'It was just high spirits,' the drummer's dad said. 'They got a bit carried away is all. I'm sure if the boys apologised . . . ?'

The policeman ignored him.

'They've had to pay good money to hire this place. At least let them get their money's worth, eh? It's only music after all. It's not as though it's going to kill anyone.'

The copper didn't seem quite so sure. I guessed he must have heard them before.

'Give the lads a chance. They need the practice.'

This raised a small smile on the policeman's face. 'I can't disagree with that.' But he got serious again all too quickly. 'Is that your son in the car outside?'

The ginger-haired dad shook his head, and pointed at the drummer. 'Gavin's my lad.'

'Well if you don't want to see him facing a charge of disturbing the peace, then I'd tell him to start packing his drums up. What do you think?' He went to join his partner outside with the singer, but as he passed me he gave me a warning look which said quite clearly he didn't want any trouble from a lanky brute like me either.

The man returned to his son, who was kneeling next to his bass drum, running his fingers around the jagged tear in its skin. I thought it was pretty cool the way his dad had stuck up for him. He reminded me of my own father.

Danny was tugging on my arm again. 'That singer was a right nutter.'

I nodded. We were both watching Gavin as he started to collect the rest of his drums from where they had fallen.

'And the band were awful,' Danny said. 'I mean, really bad.'

I nodded again. Gavin returned to inspect his bass drum, as if hoping it might have miraculously healed itself while his back was turned.

Danny nodded as well. Then said, 'But *he* was brilliant.' I wanted to say 'Told you so' now that I'd proved coming here was turning out to be worthwhile after all, but I knew how touchy Danny could be, and was just glad to have stopped him from whining. 'D'you reckon he'd want to join us?' he asked.

Gavin saw us watching him. He recognised our faces from the comp and offered us a half-hearted, 'Hello.'

'I bet he'll jump at the chance to play some decent songs,' I said. We strolled over.

Gavin's dad was helping him pack his cymbals into a circular suitcase. He looked up at us suspiciously. 'You're not more friends of that Richard Fitch, are you?'

Danny shook his head.

'Never heard of him,' I said.

'He's the young hooligan they've just carted off to the police station,' the man told us. 'Maybe they'll scare some sense into the lad.' I didn't say so, but I was thinking that Richard Fitch hadn't looked as though he was much scared of anything.

The man turned back to his son, but spoke loudly enough for Danny and me to hear. 'If I've told you once I've told you a dozen times, he's bad through and through, that one. Rotten to the core. He's had you in trouble before, I don't want him doing it again. And you know what your mother thinks of the band . . .' He shook his head. 'I've tried to help, Gavin. I've been the one shifting your gear all over town, but this has got to be the last straw. Did you hear the way that policeman talked to me?'

The drummer was still staring miserably at the hole in his drum. 'I c-can't leave the buh-buh-band,' he said, his stutter making him sound as though he were on the verge of tears.

His dad shook his head. 'I'm sorry, Gavin. But—'

'I'm starting a band,' I said, spotting my opportunity and jumping in.

Both Gavin and his dad looked up.

I grinned at the drummer. 'We thought you were great tonight, didn't we, Danny?'

Danny nodded. 'It was a brilliant solo.'

Gavin was obviously a sucker for compliments. He stood up. 'Yeah? Y-you liked it?'

We both nodded.

He shrugged shyly. 'Cheers.'

'Pity the rest of the band were so bad,' I told him, watching his face fall again. 'Absolute rubbish. Worst band in the whole world, probably. But you were brilliant. You're just what we're looking for.'

He seemed uncertain. 'What d'you m-mean?'

'We need a drummer,' I said. 'And you're the best we've seen.'

He shrugged. 'Wuh-what about the others?' he asked, looking over at one of the guitarists as he coiled up his wires.

I grinned sardonically at him. 'What about them?' I asked. 'They're not a band. They're a joke.'

He still looked unsure, but his dad stood up next to him. 'There you go, Gavin. It sounds like a good idea to me. You don't need Richard Fitch around so you can play your drums. And it will stop your mother from worrying.'

'What type of stuff do you play?' the drummer asked.

'Our own stuff,' I replied. 'Maybe play a couple of covers, but I want to stick as much as possible to our own songs.'

'I'm on guitar,' Danny put in. 'And Will sings.'

Gavin was surprised, and I knew exactly what he was thinking: a big galoot like me would probably sing like a duck. But I shrugged it off. He'd learn.

'Look,' I said. 'I'm getting together the best band around, and for that I need the best drummer around. Which is you. You can play rings around this bunch of losers and you know it.' I over-exaggerated a shrug. 'But hey, I don't want to force you. If you want to stay with this lot then it's your choice, yeah? Nothing to do with me, right? But if you want to play in a good band, the best band, then I'm asking you to join.'

Gavin looked at his dad. Then at me and Danny. And

finally at his mortally wounded drum. 'What're you called?' he asked.

'Happy,' I told him.

He looked disgusted. '*Huh-happy*? It sounds like a girls' band,' he said.

I laughed. 'So you think Shoot Cliff sounds better, do you?'

He shrugged again. 'It w-was Fitch's idea.'

I thought of the singer's home-made hairstyle. 'I don't doubt that for a minute,' I told him.

THE GUITAR

All I wanted to do was get home and play my guitar. I ran most of the way after saying 'See ya' to Danny at the top of Rothery Street.

It was exactly where I'd left it not quite two hours before, carefully propped up against the end of my bed, leaning on its strings so as not to put any extra stress on the neck, just as my father had told me. I gave its rich red body a brisk rub down with the duster first, then sat on the floor with my back to the wall and the guitar cradled in my lap. I'd only had it since the weekend, but I could already play 'Roll with It' by Oasis. Before going to sleep tonight I was determined to learn something else.

The guitar was a present from my father. He'd been home at the weekend and had saved it right up until a few minutes before he'd left on Sunday night, suddenly appearing with his suitcase in one hand and the guitar in the other. My grandma had tutted with her arms folded, scolding him for spoiling me, the same as she always did. But he hadn't taken any notice. I was used to his extravagant presents; he always brought me something when he was home, saying he was making up for not being around as much as he wanted to be. But this . . . this was fantastic.

I'd promised I'd look after it. He'd shaken my hand when his taxi had arrived and told me I'd better, it used to be his. The fact that the guitar was second-hand didn't bother me in the slightest. For me it made the instrument all the more precious, especially because my father had been the previous owner. There was a faint scratch behind the tremolo arm, and a tiny chip in the paint on the head, and I wondered exactly how they'd got there.

I can't remember telling him about my ambitions, although I don't think it would have taken him too much guessing to work it out for himself. My bedroom walls are covered in posters of different bands, pictures clipped from *Q* and the *NME*, old concert tickets, and my favourite song lyrics copied from album covers. He must have noticed the way my CD collection has grown, getting bigger in between the times he's home, sprawling across the shelves above my bed (Ash; Beatles; Beck), overflowing onto my desk (Pearl Jam; Pixies; Police), and even onto the floor (Verve; Weller; Wonderstuff). Maybe the guitar was a gentle hint to get on with it, to stop dreaming and start trying to make it happen if that's what I really wanted. Which I did. More than anything.

And I got a strange feeling whenever I held the guitar. It was a tingling, excited confidence about myself and what I wanted to do. When I held it, fingering the chords, plucking the strings, I had never felt more sure, more fearless about myself and my dreams. I couldn't play it properly yet; it was going to take a hell of a lot of practice for me to be as good as I wanted to be. But when I held that guitar, I *knew* I could make it.

I played 'Roll with It' through a couple of times, then got up to search through my CDs for another song I could teach myself. There were so many I wanted to learn, so many brilliant, brilliant songs I loved. It took me ages to decide, going through both my shelves, the stack on my desk and the pile on the floor. In the end I chose 'Just Lookin'' by the

Charlatans, mainly because it's such a cracking tune, but also because it was something Danny couldn't play just yet, and something he'd instantly recognise the moment I started playing it myself. I sat back down on the floor with my stereo's remote control by my side, flipping backwards and forwards through the track, struggling to find the right chords on my guitar. What I really needed was an amplifier to get the proper sound, but I guessed my main problem was my massive hands. Finding the right chords was a delicate business anyway, and it didn't help having sausages instead of fingers.

I'd more or less got the verse section sussed when my grandma shouted up the stairs that Beth was here. I mentally kicked myself. I'd completely forgotten I was supposed to be meeting her, and had no idea what time it was. I called back down for her to come up. By the look on her face I was well beyond simply being late.

'I thought you were coming to my house at eight,' she said. 'Do you know how long I've been waiting for you?'

'Sorry, Beth. Honest. But I've lost my watch.' I held up my naked wrists to prove it was missing.

'Why haven't you bought another one, then?' she asked.

I shrugged. 'I just couldn't find the time.'

She gave me a withering look. 'Is that meant to be funny?'

I shrugged again. But at least she wasn't scowling at me any more.

We'd first gone to the pictures together after only a week of being in the lower-sixth. Then again after two weeks. And then three. On the fourth week we went bowling, just for a change, and so had been classified as an 'item' for a little over a year now. We'd celebrated our anniversary with both the pictures *and* bowling. But that was just showing off.

Most people said we were well-matched, although I

reckoned that was because I was the only lad at school taller than her. She was six-two, but I still had a couple of extra inches somewhere between my knees and my nipples. From my point of view she was the only girl I wasn't frightened of holding. The other girls I'd been out with had all seemed too petite, too fragile, and looked as though they might break if I hugged them too hard. But Beth's height made her elegant and distinctive. Mine simply made me crack my head on low ceilings and swear a lot.

She sat herself down on my bed, taking her coat off. This was the first time I'd ever missed a date, so I knew she couldn't be too angry with me, not really. She was very pretty, probably the best-looking girl in the whole of the sixth form. She had short, blonde hair which was cut in an almost masculine style, and she liked to wear hairgrips even though she had no real need for them. She preferred the coloured plastic type, like little girls wear, and today's was bright pink with a yellow daisy on one side. She had large, green eyes and small unpierced ears. The shape of her face always made me think of an elf or a pixie, but I'd only ever tried to tell her this the once. She hadn't spoken to me for days afterwards, and I wasn't stupid.

I had no idea what she saw in me exactly. It certainly wasn't my hair, but I refused point-blank to get it cut for anyone. A couple of months ago I'd asked her what she thought was my best feature and she'd told me I had the chin of a superhero, although when I'd checked this out in the mirror it had just looked big, square, jutting and stupid to me.

'So where have you been?' she asked.

'Here,' I said. 'Playing my guitar.'

She squinted her eyes at me. 'Liar. I phoned Danny's house to see if you were there before coming round, and he said . . .'

'Oh, I get it. You've been checking up on me now, have you?'

She blushed. 'No. I just . . .'

I sat down next to her, determined to tease her. 'Don't trust me now, is that what you're saying?'

'No.'

'Wanting me on a leash, is that it? Trying to wrap me around your little finger?' I tickled her and she giggled.

'Stop it. You know that's not what I mean. It's just that you've never stood me up before . . .'

'So think yourself lucky I was willing to try it this time,' I told her.

She punched me. So I kissed her.

I wouldn't go so far as to say I loved Beth, but she was certainly great to have around. She was the best girlfriend I'd ever had. In some ways she made me the envy of the sixth form; there were plenty of lads who'd jump at the chance to take her out, Danny included.

'So, my so-called best friend grassed me up to my woman, did he?' I asked when the kiss was eventually over.

She shrugged. 'I knew you were going to see that band anyway.'

'Did he tell you what happened?'

'Not really, you know what Danny's like. He couldn't wait to get me off the phone. I think I make him nervous.'

I nodded. 'You sure as hell scare me.' I caught her punch mid-swing this time. And we kissed again.

'So you won't know our brilliant news,' I said at last.

She shook her head, then listened attentively while I told her the whole story of Shoot Cliff's ill-fated gig. She was leaning back in my arms now, and it was impossible to tell if she had ever really been angry at me at all.

'You stole their drummer?' she asked.

'I prefer to think of it as *rescued*,' I replied.

'Gavin Fisher,' she mused. 'I think he's in my dad's computer group.'

'Ginger hair and a stutter?'

She nodded. 'Yeah, that's him. My dad's forever taking the mickey out of the way he talks. Apparently he only stammers when he's not done his homework, or if he thinks he's in trouble for something.'

It was easy to forget that Beth's dad was a maths and IT teacher at the comp. You didn't expect teachers to have lives outside the classroom, never mind the best-looking daughters in the sixth form. It seemed like only a couple of years ago when I still believed they were all stored in cupboards in the staffroom at the end of the school day, with their battery packs on recharge. Luckily Mr Simmons had never taught me. Maybe if he had he would have kept his daughter well away, told her to find a nice, normal young man who didn't need to wear boats on his feet instead of shoes. After all, between them, Beth's parents were only just scraping eleven foot.

'Never heard of Robert Fitch, though,' she said.

'Richard,' I corrected.

She shook her head. 'Nor him. Is he at the comp?'

'Not that I know of.'

'He sounds like a right nutter.'

'That's just what Danny called him,' I said.

'Great minds think alike,' she grinned.

'I liked his idea about banning easy listening,' I said, remembering the scrawled posters. 'And you can't blame him for what he did.'

Beth wrinkled her nose at me.

I shrugged. 'I probably would've done the same in his position.'

'You would have started on a copper?' she scoffed. 'Yeah. I can really believe that!'

'I wouldn't have let them stop the gig,' I said sharply. 'What right have they got to throw you off the stage?'

'The right that they're the police, probably.'

But I wasn't having any of it. 'All those people have come to see you play, and you're up there on that stage in front of them, with everybody clapping and cheering. And then they come along and tell you to stop. I'd go mad if that happened to me.'

'Danny said they were rubbish anyway.'

'That's not the point,' I said angrily.

Beth held up both her hands in surrender. 'Okay, okay. I said the wrong thing, I'm sorry.' She pulled my arms tighter around her, easily smoothing things over.

'I want my band to be the best ever. It's what I want to do with my life. I want people to hear my music and have it mean something to them, like these CDs mean something to me.'

Beth nodded to prove she understood.

'All we need to get started is someone to play the bass,' I said.

'Can't you play it?' she asked.

I was confused. 'What do you mean?'

She nodded her head at my guitar. 'Can't you play bass on that?'

'That's a *lead* guitar,' I said.

'And that's different to a bass, is it?'

'Only completely,' I told her. 'Don't you know anything about music?'

'I guess not,' she admitted. 'Silly me.'

Then suddenly she sat bolt upright, popping out of my arms. 'I forgot to tell you,' she said, pulling a face. 'I think I might have dropped you in it with Danny.'

'How?'

'I'm sorry, but I didn't realise your guitar was a secret. I didn't know you hadn't told him about your dad giving it to you.'

I shrugged. 'He was going to find out sooner or later.'

'He didn't sound too pleased.'

I shook my head. 'No. I'd sort of promised him we'd only have one guitar.'

Danny was prone to acting a bit strangely sometimes. He'd virtually disowned me when Beth and I had first got together, not coming round to my house on the way to school any more, and avoiding me in the sixth-form common room. I hadn't been able to work out whether or not he was trying to punish me for seeing her, or if he simply thought that now I was in a couple, I would be spending all of my time with Beth. There were also times when I'd mention a new CD I wanted to buy, because I'd read a good review or something, and the very next day he'd appear with that exact same CD, saying he'd already got it and would copy it for me if I wanted. I've got to admit he's done that particular trick so often I've once or twice just mentioned a CD knowing he'd buy it and I'd end up getting a freebie.

I guess the reason I hadn't told him about the guitar was because I knew it might cause a couple of problems. He'd had a guitar for a few years now, but still hadn't learned how to play it properly. Whenever I saw it it was in the corner of his bedroom being used as a coat-stand. Although, to be fair, it had been his idea to start a band. He'd mentioned it two or three times over the summer. 'It'll be great, Will. You singing, me on guitar. We'd ask if we could play a gig at Swift's and everything.'

Getting a band together had been exactly what I'd wanted to do as well. But it hadn't been until I'd got my hands on my father's old guitar and I'd felt that tingling, excited confidence in my belly that I'd known for definite I could make it happen.

As soon as I'd touched the guitar, even before my dad's taxi had arrived, I'd known exactly what we should call ourselves. I'd pictured the scene perfectly in my head: the rest of the band would be on the stage behind me, instruments ready, and I'd walk up to the microphone, the lights bright and hot, the buzz of nerves and anticipation, all the audience clapping and cheering, shouting for us to play their favourite songs. I'd stare down at them all from the front of the stage.

'Good evening, ladies and gentlemen,' I'd say. 'We are Happy. And we hope you are too!'

'So where are you going to find someone to play bass, then?' Beth asked. 'I guess you can't get them free in a box of Frosties these days.'

I laughed, pulling her towards me again. 'Guess not, no. Danny says his sister's boyfriend can play, but we'll have to find out if he's interested first. And audition him, of course.'

'Of course.'

My head was full of visions again. I could see the audience and hear the applause. 'I've written the lyrics to three songs already, you know? I just need to try and work out some tunes now.'

She nodded her head gently, tapping the back of it against my chest, nestling into my arms.

'I've called them "Everything You Want to Hear", "Frozen Gold" and "Stay On".'

'You've told me,' she said. 'About a hundred times.'

'Did I tell you what we're going to call ourselves?'

She nodded again. 'About a thousand times.'

'Can you imagine it? Will Brown and Danny Graham on *Top of the Pops*?'

'What about Beth Simmons?' she asked.

I frowned. 'What do you mean?'

'All I've heard you talk about for the past few days is how famous and adored you and Danny are going to be.' She twisted in my arms to look me in the face. 'What about me?' she said. 'You never mention my name. Is there any room for me in this wonderful future of yours?'

I shrugged. I didn't know what to say. To be honest, I hadn't really thought about it. But I mended it all with a kiss. A kiss so big I began to worry about getting friction burns on my tongue.

'LET'S ROCK!'

It was a full week since the night at the scout hut, and Danny and I had got to know Gavin pretty well over the past few days. The three of us hung around together at school, making plans, talking band-talk. I liked him a lot, he'd become a friend. And right now he had chrysanthemums in his hair.

'Hey, look. I'm a hippy.'

I shook my head at him, smiling sadly. 'No, Gav. You're a moron.'

'Stop messing about, will you, Gav?' Danny said. 'My mum'll kill me if you do anything to her flowers.'

Danny's mum and dad owned the flower shop on Cuffe Street, C and E Florists, next to the Chinese takeaway. He'd somehow managed to persuade them to let us use the back room on the promise that we cleared up after ourselves and didn't damage any of the flowers. He must have done some heavy begging to get them to agree; his dad wasn't so bad, but his mother could act like a right cow when the mood struck her. The smell of so many flowers in such a confined space was sickly-sweet. But the light was dim, the room damp with a bare concrete floor, and the obscurity of the location was just enough to make things feel like almost proper rock 'n' roll.

My grandad had lent me the money to buy an amplifier and a microphone (I'd promised to pay him back, although I wasn't sure exactly how I planned to do it just yet, seeing as I didn't have a job and relied on my grandparents for money anyhow), but I hadn't been able to get myself a stand as well. I had to use a length of blue ribbon to suspend the microphone from one of the overhead lights. The problem was I couldn't quite get it to hang at the right height for my mouth. It was a beautiful microphone, though, one of those old-fashioned ones, like the old singers used to have back in the sixties or something. Admittedly, if I'd bought a normal mike I would have also been able to buy a stand for it, but this one had simply been too cool to refuse.

'What's this guy like, then?' I asked Danny, as I climbed on and off a stool to hang and re-hang my microphone.

'You've met him,' he told me. 'At my dad's fiftieth birthday party.'

We were talking about his sister's boyfriend, Ian Holmes; our bass player, hopefully. He hadn't exactly been our first choice of bassist, more like our only choice, because none of us knew anyone else who could play. Gavin had suggested his mate from Shoot Cliff, but he'd turned out to be too pally with Richard Fitch to want to get involved with us. So, in the end, it had to be Ian or nothing.

'I can't remember him,' I said. 'But he can definitely play, yeah?'

'Oh, yeah.' Danny nodded quickly. 'Of course. His uncle teaches bass or something, and taught him. Deborah reckons he's excellent.'

I nodded, but didn't say anything. The fact that this guy was Deborah's boyfriend was already a black mark against him in my book. There was no love lost between my friend's elder sister and me. She'd always thought I was a bit of a brat, a bit spoilt, although she'd only say as much when my back was turned. Personally, I didn't care which way she was facing when I told people she was a snob. She probably hated me because I'd nicknamed her 'The Tractor' (small wheels up front, massive at the rear).

'He's been playing since he was about ten,' Danny informed me, but again I only nodded.

'What're these called?' Gavin asked, prodding petals.

'Halitosis,' Danny told him.

He looked pleased. 'Cool. I think my mum's got some in the living room.'

Earlier on he'd found a dwarf sunflower with huge yellow petals in a little purple pot. It was the one Danny's mum used to decorate the shop and wasn't meant for sale. He'd picked it up while Danny wasn't looking and put it inside his new bass drum. It was quite funny really (and just like Gav) that he'd bought a new drum after that copper had put a hole in the old one, but this new drum already had a hole in it anyway, and a bigger one at that too, the difference being that the manufacturer had made this hole, and it was meant to be there. Apparently. The bass drum is the one which faces out at the audience, and most bands have their name or logo printed on the skin for everyone to see. That had been my original idea for Gavin's new drum as well, but he obviously thought the sunflower looked better. He'd positioned the plant just inside the manufactured hole, with its big, bright yellow head poking out. And every time he pedalled his new drum the sunflower shook its petals in time to the beat.

I finally managed to get my microphone to hang down at the correct height, and turned my attention to my guitar. Beth had bought me a black leather carry-case for it as a late anniversary present, and to say thank you I'd got Danny to deliver her a bouquet of flowers because I knew how much she loved them. He was hovering over me as I unzipped the case, even though he'd already been round to my house twice to have a look at it, and then a third time to have a go.

As predicted, he'd been in a mood about it to begin with. The day after Beth had told him about it on the phone he'd not stopped by on his way to school that morning. I'd arrived late because I'd been waiting for him, and he'd already shot off to the first lesson. It was his way of punishing me for daring to want to play guitar as well as him, but I knew he'd come round soon enough. It had only taken him until dinner time before he'd started speaking to me again.

He'd picked a few faults with it when he did turn up to have a look. He'd claimed the neck was too thick, didn't feel right, and he didn't like the action (which is apparently the gap between the strings and the fretboard). To be honest, he may very well have been right, seeing as it was the first guitar I'd ever tried to play. But if it had been good enough for my father, then I reckoned my friend was very probably talking out of his backside.

'I've decided to get a new guitar,' he told me as I slipped the strap over my shoulder.

I raised my eyebrows at him. 'Yeah?'

He nodded quickly. 'Yeah. I mean, my guitar's fine, I love it, but it is beginning to look a bit battered. *I've* been playing for three years, don't forget.' He watched me plug in and turn on my amp. 'I was thinking, what if I get a red one too? Not the same as yours, obviously. But it'd look smart if we both had the same colour, wouldn't it?'

'Sounds great,' I said. 'You'll have to let me come with you when you're choosing it.'

He nodded vigorously. 'Great. Yeah. Definitely.' He grabbed his own, admittedly battered guitar, full of enthusiasm again. 'I'll get my mum to give me some extra shifts before Christmas. I'll save up loads.'

I grinned back. I knew I could be mean to him sometimes,

but he was still my oldest and closest friend. And I loved him to bits really.

I think his main concern was that I might want to steal all the glory; not only was I the singer and frontman of this band, but maybe I wanted to do all the fancy guitar-work as well? He just wanted some attention for himself, which was fine by me. I wasn't interested in all the technical musician-ship stuff anyway; all I wanted was to write and sing some decent songs. Some great songs.

Ian arrived late. He hurried in looking flustered, his glasses misting up in the damp warmth of the little back room.

'Apologies, everyone,' he said. 'I got trapped in a meeting and couldn't get away until a few minutes ago.' He worked for the Royal Bank of Scotland, and was still wearing his suit and tie.

'That's okay,' Danny said, then quickly introduced him to me and Gavin. He walked over and shook hands with us both. Gavin seemed a bit shocked by the gesture, as if he'd never done it before. He stuttered his hello, then pulled the daffodils out from down the front of his jeans and retreated behind his drums, looking embarrassed.

'We met at Mr Graham's birthday, if you remember?' I said, shaking Ian's hand firmly.

He may have been four years older, but I was four inches taller. 'That's right. But I recognise you from all the voodoo dolls Deborah keeps making. She's got a shelf full. Not had any accidents recently, have you? Caught any nasty diseases?'

I laughed. 'Not yet,' I said.

'That will disappoint her. But take no notice,' he told me. 'I'll soon slap her into line.' Then added quickly, 'No offence, Danny.'

Danny shook his head to prove there was none taken, but gave me a sly, knowing glance. He'd already let slip that Ian was completely smitten with his sister, and in reality she had him wrapped around her chubby little finger.

I warmed to the older lad straight away, and wondered how on the earth the Tractor had managed to get her hooks into him. I instantly knew that if he was as good a bass player as Danny kept assuring me, then we'd be firm friends for sure.

Ian set his gear up in the far corner of the room, in front of the bench used to make up the bouquets for delivery, carefully removing any wet cuts of stem or scrap cellophane before allowing his amp to sit there. He hung his jacket on the back of the door, didn't take his tie off, but loosened it slightly by undoing the top button of his shirt. He rolled his sleeves up to his elbows, slung his big blue bass around his shoulder and pushed his glasses up his nose.

'Let's rock!' he said, making the rest of us burst out laughing again.

We started by pretending to tune up. I say 'pretending' because what we were really doing was the musician's version of marking his territory. Lions and tigers pee on rocks or bushes; guitarists lay down the trickiest riffs they know.

I was standing by the shop doorway, picking out a solo I'd learned especially. Danny was just to my left along the back wall with buckets of carnations at his feet. He was watching me carefully. He was playing some complicated piece I didn't recognise. Ian surrounded himself with roses, tulips and a fat, funky rhythm. And even Gavin was thundering out a stuttering, syncopated beat, with the sunflower shaking its big, yellow head. In short, we were all showing off, all weighing each other up. But we were all playing different songs, all keeping different time, and it must have sounded like a train crash to Mr Li and his customers next door.

After about fifteen minutes of this things were getting well out of hand, and we were scraping the intolerable Shoot Cliff levels of cacophony. I shouted through my microphone to quieten everyone down. I was using an old practice amp of Danny's for the mike, seeing as we didn't have a proper PA system for it at the minute, and it was nowhere near loud enough for the others to hear me above their own din. I had to put my guitar down and tap each of them on the shoulder before they'd shut up. Even so Gavin's shoulder needed tapping twice. And then punching. (This was soon to become one of our drummer's familiar traits, and in subsequent practices I discovered that the only way to actually make him shut up was to confiscate his sticks.)

'Nice to see we're all so enthusiastic,' I said with the merest hint of sarcasm. 'But maybe we should get started properly, yeah?'

'Let's start with something we all know,' Danny offered.

But I shook my head. 'If we start off by playing other people's songs,' I said, 'then we'll *always* be playing other people's songs. I want to start with something brand new, something of our own. Everybody agree?'

Nobody said they disagreed.

'I've written this tune,' I told them. 'Or the basic chorus part to it anyway. I'll play it through a couple of times, and then you three join in when you know what's happening. See if we can come up with anything interesting. Okay?'

They all looked a bit vague, but I was determined to jump in at the deep end. And far too impatient not to.

This 'tune' of mine was really just a couple of chords I'd stolen from 'Roll with It', and a couple more from 'Just Lookin'', simply strung together in a different order. But I thought it sounded pretty good, and guessed that a lot of proper songs were probably written in the same fashion anyway. I felt slightly self-conscious with the three of them watching my sausage fingers and played a bum chord to begin with. Then I told myself to get a grip, and strummed out the snappy little tune I'd been working on for the past couple of days instead of doing my homework.

I admit it wasn't exactly spectacular or ground-breaking, but it had a jolly, kind of up-beat feel to it. I played it through twice with the other three watching me, nobody really wanting to make the first move. So I played it again. Then once more before Gavin at last started quietly tapping out a steady beat on his snare drum and hi-hat cymbal. I immediately turned to him to urge him into picking it up a little. He was bobbing his head to mark time.

Ian and Danny stayed quiet, but Gavin was clearly beginning to enjoy himself. He started hitting his snare that tiny bit harder, lifting the sound. He moved to his cymbals once, then again. I was nodding at him, smiling, encouraging. And now Ian had plucked up enough courage to join in. He picked out a steady, sensible rhythm. He hunched over his bass, tapped his foot, and the volume rose.

Danny was the only one not playing. He was watching my fingers, following where they went on the fretboard, watching for the changes. I stepped over to him and held my guitar up a little to show him the chord shapes. He tried to copy them, looking hesitant, checking my fingers, checking his. I grinned at him, raising my eyebrows. He smiled back. The volume rose again.

Ian tapped his foot harder. He weaved his bass line in and out of the two guitars, forgetting the sensible bit, his fingers running up and down the fretboard. And I started singing.

Snatches of lyrics jumped into my head. 'I was chasing summer the other day . . . Oh, I wonder, where is summer . . . ?' My microphone swung slightly on the blue ribbon in front of me.

Danny was attacking his guitar now, chasing me chord for chord, strumming hard, really going for it. He experimented with a short solo, keeping within my chords, but rising above them to pick out the melody. He must have been practising when I wasn't looking. He was grinning like a loon.

The rest of us followed, and the volume rose again.

Gavin was thumping out the beat on his bass drum. The sunflower inside banged its big, yellow head. He seemed to let his sticks go, rolled the sound around the whole of his kit. He used every drum in turn. His crashing cymbals sounded like exclamation marks. And Ian was stomping his foot to keep time now. The look on his face made me wonder if he needed the toilet, but his fingers made the bass line dance. They flew across the frets.

And the volume rose again.

We were all grinning now, all bopping our heads along with Gavin's sunflower. Danny, Ian and I gradually moved out from our separate corners to gather around the drummer and his kit, looping the tune around and around. It was as if there had been a spark in the back room of C and E Florists, and now there was a definite fire. Our grins glowed. We were playing real music to warm the damp, little room.

I've often thought about artists in the past, and about writers, about what it must be like to feel the inspiration and creativity pouring out as you fill the the canvas with paint or the page with words. I've always believed it must be such an uplifting experience. But then they only ever have themselves to share that feeling with, because painting and writing by their very nature are lonely activities. In this little room, however, there were four of us all sharing and all experiencing that feeling. This was creativity times four. The sweet scented air was our canvas, the dim light our paper, and we filled it with *our* music. And we filled it four times over.

We played on and on, none of us wanting the feeling to stop. We played faster. We were all sweating. I could feel it on my forehead, and tried to blink it away as it ran into my eyes. My fat fingers were killing me, the tips of them burning. But I couldn't stop. We all played our fair share of bum notes, or struggled to correct missed changes, but who cared? Not me. Not Danny or Gavin or Ian. We laughed at each other, none of it seeming to matter as the energy of our playing carried us on and on.

Gavin grinned at Ian. Ian passed it on to me. I turned to Danny and nodded in confirmation. We were a band now.

And the sunflower bopped and boogied its head.

THE FOUR OF US

We were celebrating. Ian had bought a crate of cheap Belgian beer, and Danny, Gavin and I were helping him drink it. The four of us were sprawled across Danny's living-room furniture refusing to be entertained by *Top of the Pops*. We abused all of the teenie-bop cack, we belched loudly through some inane boy-band video, we even hurled swear words and scrunched-up crisp packets at a diabolical dance act calling themselves Boom Baby 101, or some such nonsense.

'Do you know what would be really offensive?' I asked. 'What would really, really naff me off?' I prodded a finger at the screen. 'If whichever record company signed *them*, refused to sign *us*! Now wouldn't that be just like a kick in the teeth?'

Everybody nodded.

'A kick in the goolies,' Gavin expanded.

'A turd in your swimming pool,' Danny offered.

'A hairy dog's head in your mother's wardrobe,' Ian said.

We all looked at him, then howled with laughter. I think the drink was getting to us.

We were celebrating getting our first gig. Danny and I had been to see the manager of Swift's earlier in the day. It was the best nightclub in Cleeston, the only place to go for decent music, and one of the few places which still let live bands play. The manager was a small, grey-haired bloke with glasses who looked more like the short one out of *The Two Ronnies* than the owner of the coolest club in town, but he gave us the provisional date of December 6th, a Thursday night. He said he really needed to hear a tape of us playing before he could make it a solid booking, so we'd decided to record one of our rehearsals for him to listen to. We wouldn't get paid because it was our first gig, but he'd promised that if we were good enough he'd want us back in the new year. I've got to admit, however, that none of the details really mattered; just the fact that we were playing a gig, and playing it at Swift's, was enough for the celebration. In my opinion we should really have been drinking champagne, but I reckoned we would have plenty of time after the gig for that.

Now at least, we had something to aim for. Our first gig, Thursday December 6th. Which gave us exactly a day under seven weeks to rehearse and get ready. Not a lot of time, but we had all the confidence in the world . . . if not more.

'D'you think we're good enough, then?' Gavin asked. 'To get a record deal?'

Danny nodded his head so hard I thought it might fall off. 'Definitely,' he said, waving his bottle. 'No doubt about it. Wouldn't you agree, Will?'

'Absolutely,' I told him, chinking my bottle against his.

And the four of us sat there grinning inanely at each other. *Top of the Pops* came to an end and we all cheered.

'Put some decent music on, Danny,' Ian told him. And Danny was over at his parents' stereo in a flash, ferreting through their CD collection, wrinkling his nose at the contents.

'I better get going,' Gavin told us. He pushed himself out of the settee. 'Can I have my shoes, Danny?'

'Where're you off to?' Danny asked, disappointed the drummer was leaving. This was meant to be a celebration, a 'band night'.

Gavin shrugged. 'Just . . . just m-meeting someone.' The stutter instantly gave his game away.

I shook my head in disbelief. 'Another one? How'd you do it, Gav? You must have a waiting list or something.'

'No, just muscles,' Ian told us with a grin.

Gavin blushed, his cheeks clashing with his hair. He looked awkward in the sudden glare of our attention. He'd let slip at our last rehearsal that one of the main reasons he wanted to be a drummer was because girls loved lads who were in a band. He'd said they went for drummers especially, because drummers were (and I quote), 'The backbone of the band. The powerhouse which everybody else relied on. And the ones with the most muscles.' Which was why he always took his shirt off when he played.

Obviously we'd all taken the mick. But this was the third girl in a fortnight!

'What's this one called?' Danny asked.

Gavin touched his ear self-consciously, then rubbed his bristly red hair. 'L-L-Lisa,' he mumbled.

Ian seemed confused. 'Eh? Lisa?' He gave the drummer a quizzical look. 'Are you sure? I thought you said it was Sarah tonight?'

Gavin looked confused too. 'Did I?'

Ian nodded emphatically. 'Yep. You definitely told me it was Sarah's lucky night tonight.'

But I shook my head. 'No, you're wrong,' I said. 'It's Friday, right? You told me you were seeing Melissa on Friday.'

Gavin turned from Ian to me. Then back again. He looked suddenly anxious. 'Sss-top m-messing about.' He swapped hands to rub his head with his left one now, while Ian and I continued to argue over girls' names.

'He told me it was Sarah.'

'I don't care what he told you. When I spoke to him yesterday he said . . .'

Gavin was standing between the two of us, twisting on his heel to keep track. Danny thought it was so funny he had tears in his eyes. Gav kept trying to speak, but we wouldn't let him. Panic twitched at the corner of his mouth and made his eyes wide and comic, highlighted by the alcohol. People didn't usually pick on Gavin. He may not have been very tall, but he was twice as wide as most kids. Now, however, he was muddled and drunk. He looked like a plump, ginger rabbit, not sure whether it was easier to be eaten for dinner or to be run over by a fast car. And Danny thought it was the most hilarious thing he had ever seen. In fact, he laughed so hard he spilled beer all over his mother's living-room carpet.

I saw it happen. I shouted, 'Danny! Watch what you're . . . !' But I was too late. One second he was holding the bottle tightly and firmly, enjoying the show, and the next he was watching in terror as it disgorged a flood of golden-brown liquid all over his mother's best carpet. The puddle fizzed softly around the edges as it soaked in.

'OH MY GOD!' he shrieked, leaping to his feet. 'Quick! Quick! *Do* something!'

There was a moment's pause, a short, two-beat rest before Gavin and Ian realised what was going on, and before I could see through the alcoholic fog which had descended on my mind. Then all four of us were on our feet, shouting and running around. Even Gavin, who'd never met the woman, knew about Danny's mother – the legend had spread. None of us needed telling what she'd do if she came home to find beer stains on her best carpet.

We'd all been sitting abusing the television in our socks because she didn't allow anyone to wear shoes in the house, and ours were placed neatly side by side on the rack in the cupboard underneath the stairs. She hoovered twice a day, once before she went to work and once when she returned home. Danny had admitted to me a few years ago that he had often wondered exactly who the mysterious person was who broke in during the day to spread dust and filth throughout his house when everybody else was out. His mother had been known to follow people from the kitchen to the bathroom to the bedroom with a cloth to clean their fingerprints from door handles. Mr Graham told stories about her having shares in Mr Sheen. She polished the fruit in the bowl. And added to this, the fact that this particular carpet had been her birthday present only three months ago, I think our reaction was more than justified.

But I couldn't seem to get myself to think straight. It was either the panic or the alcohol (or both) making me stand there and shout, 'Do something! Quick! Do something!' without actually doing anything myself. I stared as the puddle grew and grew. Who would have thought so little a bottle could hold so much beer?

'Cloth! Get a cloth!' Ian was shouting. He ran towards the kitchen with Danny quick to follow him. And at last I could move too. I did the first thing that came into my foggy head. I stepped into the puddle. Gavin joined me and we paddled together trying to soak up as much into our socks as we could. I could feel the beer cold and wet on the soles of my feet, between my toes.

The other two came charging back into the room clutching tea towels and with a thick, white streamer of Dixel kitchen roll flying out behind them.

'What are you doing?' Ian bellowed at us incredulously. 'Get out of the way!'

I fell backwards into the armchair lifting my soaking feet high in the air. But Gavin walked over to the settee, leaving wet footprints all the way. Danny wailed and shoved him down, ordering him to get his socks off. Ian was on his hands and knees with the tea towels. I was watching as if in a daze. Danny's mum was going to kill us. How could we explain what had happened? Making a mess of her carpet was going to be bad enough, but making a mess of her carpet with alcohol was going to be so very, very much worse. It didn't bear thinking about. Gavin was shoving his socks in the plastic carrier bag which held our empty bottles, Ian was on his second tea towel, and Danny had just about used up all of the kitchen roll. I couldn't get the image of Mrs Graham's dreaded face from out of my head. We were deader than vinyl. She was going to be so mad she might even stop us from using the back room of her shop . . .

The thought was a sharp, instantly sobering slap in my face.

'Get some more cloths,' Ian shouted. I realised that if we got caught he was going to be next in line after Danny for the blame. He was the one buying drinks for minors, and I'm sure his girlfriend's parents weren't going to be very pleased about that.

And I was concerned for him, I really, truly was. But I could see our rehearsal room being taken from us, and stopping that from happening was the most important thing in the world right now.

'Bathroom,' Danny was shouting at me. 'Get some towels from the bathroom!'

I whipped off my soggy socks and flung them in the carrier bag with Gavin's, then ran upstairs to get a towel from Danny's bathroom. I was telling God that if He got us out of this then I was going to be a good person from now on and would never do anything bad for the rest of my life, honest. But I don't think He believed me (and I don't think I can blame Him). My great, lanky legs got tangled up on the stairs and I keeled over, coming down hard and painfully on one knee, and took His name in vain very loudly. I was yanking the towels off the rail on the wall when I heard a car pulling up in the driveway and knew Danny's parents were home far earlier than they should have been.

I hurtled down the stairs with the bath towels in my arms. The others had heard the car too. Ian snatched the towels off me and rubbed so hard at the carpet I thought he was going to wear it away. Gavin was collecting the already soaking tea towels and stuffing them in the plastic bag. Danny was wailing like a baby. The place stank like a brewery.

I grabbed Danny. 'Where's your air freshener?'

He shook his head. 'I don't know. I don't know.' His eyes were wide with terror.

'We've got to get rid of the smell,' I told him. 'What about your deodorant?'

'My room,' he said, staring at the still so-very-obvious stain. 'Next to my bed.'

I ran back up the stairs, my knee throbbing.

'And bring you and Gav some more socks,' Ian called after me.

I didn't dare turn the light on in Danny's room and had to fumble in the dark for his can of Lynx Oriental and two pairs of socks. I managed a glance out of the window to see his mother holding open the garage door for his dad to drive the car in. If the weather report hadn't threatened rain earlier then maybe he would have left it out in the drive all night. I got the feeling that the weather girl was on my side even if God wasn't.

I tripped and stumbled in my haste to get back down the stairs and into the living room. I threw Gavin a pair of clean socks. Then pushed Ian out of the way and virtually emptied the can of deodorant onto the damp patch. Ian took the bag with the soaking, stinking socks and towels through into the kitchen and left it just outside the back door for him to collect on his way out. He came back and hurriedly handed around a pack of Polos to mask our breath. I'd just managed to get my own pair of fresh socks on when I heard the front door open. Danny jumped to sit on the beer stain.

I was expecting his mother, but instead it was Mr Graham who poked his head round the living-room door. He was greeted by the sight of the four of us sitting like statues in front of the TV.

Danny cleared his throat and tried to arrange the four or five Polos he'd stuffed in his mouth so he could speak properly.

'You're back early,' he said hesitantly, with a fixed smile, looking so unbelievably guilty.

'I don't think it was exactly your mother's type of film,' his dad said. He stepped into the room, taking his glasses off and polishing the lenses on the front of his shirt. 'She didn't appreciate the language. You know what she's like.'

Danny nodded obediently.

I liked Mr Graham, I liked him a lot. He'd been good to me over the years, helped me out when my own father was away, and for that I'd always be grateful. But right now I knew I just wanted him to go away and leave us alone.

He didn't. He stayed in the doorway cleaning his glasses. He was actually the same age as my father, but looked a good deal older. It was probably his grey hair. My father's was still thick and dark, and long enough to be worn in a ponytail. My father wore leather jackets and jeans, whereas I'd never seen Mr Graham in anything other than a shirt and trousers, often with a tie.

'So what've you lads been up to?' he asked. 'Have you managed to work out how to be famous yet?'

We all shrugged at him. Danny shuffled on his backside next to me and I wanted to tell him to keep still for God's sake.

'I hope you realise I'm going to start charging you to hire out the back room of my shop the minute you're at number one,' Mr Graham said.

We all laughed at him, much too loudly. We laughed long and hard. Gavin even slapped his thigh, making me cringe inwardly. I noticed he'd put the clean pair of socks on inside out and felt my heart tighten painfully in my chest. I almost choked on my mouthful of Polos. But luckily Danny's dad didn't seem to notice (or if he did he maybe thought that that kind of thing was only to be expected from Gav). He smiled at us, enjoying his moment of comedy. And I was willing him to leave. I was asking God to set off his car alarm or some-thing.

Suddenly a frown fell across the man's face. He sniffed, and wrinkled his brow. He scratched his greying head. I caught myself wondering if we could get him out of the room by using sheer force. He wasn't as tall as me or as wide as Gavin, so maybe we could overpower him and throw him out of his own living room, toss him into the hallway and bar the door. I realised it was the beer making me think like that, but the idea did seem rather promising at the time.

His frown deepened slightly. Or was it my imagination? He put his glasses back on. He stepped further into the room, coming round the side of the settee. 'Who's the one with all the aftershave?' he asked.

None of us knew what to say. We all looked at each other, and could all read the look of fear in each other's eyes. The two or three seconds of silence stretched out like elastic. Then stretched out some more. Danny opened his mouth to say something, but I was sure he had no idea what on earth it was going to be. I saw the flower shop's little back room disappearing down the plug hole, gurgling away for ever and ever . . .

And suddenly I said, 'Blame Ian.' Everybody looked at me. 'He's meeting Deborah later. After she's finished work.' The lie was so easy, so fluid. I impressed myself.

Ian looked shocked. He turned slowly from me to Mr Graham. His expression changed almost mechanically and he grinned up idiotically at the man. He was suddenly reduced from a twenty-one-year-old young man with a good job and steady income to a little kid who's been caught looking up rude words in the dictionary.

'You must have had a bath in the stuff,' Mr Graham said.

And all Ian could do was grin.

Mr Graham shook his head in a tutting, 'youth-of-today' kind of way. He turned to leave us. 'Your mother and I will be going over the shop's books in the dining room,' he said to Danny. 'Try and keep the noise down, okay? Your mother's feeling delicate.'

Danny said he would. Absolutely. No problem there. I felt my chest loosen more and more the closer his dad got to the door, and could tell the same was happening to my friends as we all urged him on with every step. We sat silently watching him retreat further across the room, sucking hard on our Polos.

But he stopped halfway through the door. He turned round to look at us and we each held our breath, not daring to move a single muscle which could somehow give us away.

'Do any of you want a drink?' he asked.

'No!' we all shouted in a single, clear voice.

THE MUSIC SHOP

Had I died and gone to Heaven?

I had to duck my head and dodge in between all the guitars hanging in rows from the little shop's walls. I turned in a slow circle; I was surrounded by them, everywhere I looked. Tanglewood, Rickenbacker, Washburn and Fender; names like magic charms. The paintwork shone, the tuning pegs sparkled. And the best feeling of all, the one that mattered most, was that I could pick any one of them, reach down whichever one I chose, and conjure a tune out of it. Even better – one of *my* tunes.

Danny was next to me. He'd saved up seventy-five pounds, enough to lay down a deposit for the new guitar he wanted. It would have been a round hundred but he'd decided to buy his mum a rug for Christmas to cover the stain on her living-room carpet. Personally I thought it was hardly noticeable, but Danny swore blind his mum would spot it one of these days. He stood next to me staring up at the rows of guitars, his mouth open and his eyes wide, his money hot enough to be burning a hole in his pocket. The thought of buying himself a new guitar had made him forget how upset he was supposed to be with me for wanting to play one too.

Beth was also with us. I wanted to hold her hand, but she wouldn't take it out of her pocket.

'This place is fantastic,' I said.

She only smiled briefly, not quite getting the point. She

was in a weird mood today. Not that it was anything new, she'd been acting all sulky and miserable for the past couple of weeks now. I had no idea what was the matter.

'You can bury me here when I die,' I told her.

She shook her head at me. 'God, Will,' she said. 'They're only guitars.'

Which made both Danny and me laugh at her. But not nastily.

Danny moved down the middle of the narrow shop, trying to see all of the guitars on either side of him at once. He could have been gazing at naked women, the curves of a guitar's body mimicking that of a woman's.

The guy behind the counter was wearing a bandana and a Harley-Davidson T-shirt which only just covered his beer belly. He spotted us from the far end of the shop and hurried over, having instantly recognised the look on Danny's face. It was the look of a greedy kid in a chocolate factory.

'After anything in particular?' he asked. He gestured at the beautiful, ruby-red Gibson Danny's eyes had finally come to rest on. 'Could mebbe do you an offer on that,' he said. 'Try it out if you want. Got a spare amp laid around you could plug into.'

Danny nodded quickly. 'Yeah, please. That'd be great.' He grinned at me as if it were already Christmas, and we watched eagerly as the owner carefully reached the guitar down for us.

Beth might not have been able to understand the significance, but for me, being able to play the guitar was already halfway towards being a rock star, basically because it is such a magical, sexy, rock-star instrument. Not only is it the main ingredient for the songs, but it also makes you look good when you play it. It's not like a tuba or a flute, is it? It's such a flattering instrument. And it's not like the piano which hides you from your audience. A guitar is what you always play in front of the wardrobe mirror. No offence to Gavin, but you don't exactly mime the drums to your favourite record turned up full blast when you're alone in your bedroom (although maybe *he* does). Nine out of ten people who want to be in a band want to either sing or play the guitar. Or both. And so it was in my case too.

Things were going great for us at the moment, couldn't have been better. We were rehearsing twice a week now, and I'd written three new songs. The blisters on my fingertips from all the practising I was doing had finally burst and the skin was starting to harden over nicely. Beth hated them, said they felt horrible. But Danny, Ian and I agreed they were the sign of a true guitarist, and that all professional players had them. (It was a ritual to compare callouses at every rehearsal.) We all also agreed that Gavin's sunflower looked really cool and it should be our mascot. I'd decided we should use it as our logo on posters, T-shirts and even on the cover of our first album. I thought the image of a sunflower summed up Happy perfectly.

It may sound silly, but I reckoned one of the reasons things were going so well was because I'd stopped playing the lottery. My father had told me once that you only ever get three wishes in life, just like the fairy stories always say, and that you should never waste them. I'd decided that the lottery was actually using up one of my wishes, because every week I was wishing I would win. So I'd stopped playing, and now could aim all three of my wishes at Happy. And it seemed to be working so far.

I'd talked to my father on the phone the other night, hardly letting him get a word in edgeways because I'd wanted to tell him everything I could about the band and about how much guitar practice I was doing. He'd said he was really proud of me, told me to keep up the good work, and had promised to come home to see our gig at Swift's if he wasn't working. It made me kind of nervous to think that he would be watching me up on that stage, especially seeing as I'd be using his guitar. But it made me all the more excited about the gig as well. If he'd said he was proud of me when all I was doing was talking about playing, I couldn't wait to hear what he said when he could actually *see* me play.

I'm very lucky, I know that. Most kids seem to hate their parents nowadays, but my father and I always get on brilliantly whenever he's home. Danny once said I only liked him because he always brought me presents back with him – expensive ones like the widescreen TV, or the video and the massive stereo I've got in my bedroom. It's not true. We've got a special relationship exactly because of the distance between us. He doesn't have to worry about disciplining me, he doesn't have to give me grief because I won't eat my greens or because I left my bike out in the rain. He leaves all of that kind of stuff to my grandparents. He's never had to punish me, so I've never had to hate him. We're more like friends.

My mother died when I was very young, and I don't really remember her. I like to think I do; I've seen hundreds of pictures of her and know exactly what she looked like. I'm sure I have this memory of her pushing my pram through the park at the bottom of Wollston Hill. Sometimes I think I even remember the sound of the ducks on the pond, and that it was a summer's day. My father said it can't be a proper memory though, because we lived in London until she died, and she had never actually set foot in Cleeston, never mind the park at the bottom of Wollston Hill. So maybe it was another park in London somewhere, I don't know. I do know she's smiling in the memory, but then again I've only ever seen her in my grandma's old photographs and she's always smiling in them. So to be honest, I don't even know what she looks like when she's sad, or angry, or sleeping, or drunk. Which I guess proves once again how lucky I am. It's good to only ever think of your mum when she's smiling.

I live with my grandparents because my father has to constantly travel all over the world to get work. He comes back as often as he can, phones every month if he won't be home, sends postcards when he's got time. I don't mind living with Grandma and Grandad; they let me do more or less what I please. I suppose some kids might have ended up being right sad cases if their mother was dead and their father couldn't always be around, but I've always been too big to be picked on by other kids, and too big to need sympathy from adults. Although that's the only decent thing there is about being as big as me – most of the time I hate it. Being six foot five has been the bane of my life so far.

People always make assumptions about you if you're tall – it's worse than wearing glasses. They think you're either a thug or a goon, or both; you're either going to beat them up or trip over your own great, big, clumsy feet. Little kids and old ladies stare at you as if you're a freak. Of course, thanks to Happy, I'm going to prove them all wrong.

The music-shop guy handed the gorgeous red guitar to Danny, who held it like the crown jewels. His cheeks reflected the deep blush of the paintwork. He slipped the strap over his shoulder.

'Feels fantastic,' he said in a whisper, grinning at me.

'The amp's in the back somewhere,' the owner said and wandered off to find it, his baggy jeans giving him a bum-cleavage as bad as any builder's.

Danny tested out a few chord shapes on the highly polished neck, and plucked at the string tentatively. He looked nervous holding it. He looked like a chump.

I laughed at him. 'Let's have a go,' I said, and took the

guitar from him. He was right, it really did feel fantastic. I played the opening couple of bars to one of our songs, 'Chasing Summer'. 'Nice action,' I told him.

I started to sing along with my playing, just quietly at first. But I noticed the shop's owner was watching me from the back of the shop, so I raised my voice. I played and sang the whole of the song from start to finish with Danny, Beth and the owner listening.

I've got a great voice, you see. And I know it's great. Every year I get picked to do all the solos in the comp's Christmas carol concert (except this year I've got more important things going on). When I was younger I used to make tapes of myself singing and give them to my grandma for her birthday, sometimes to Danny's mum, too. They both said I sang like an angel. (And my father once told me I sounded like *they'd* dropped when I was eight, although it took me a few years before I'd realised it was a compliment.) Even Beth had thought it was strange when she first heard me sing. She'd said she was really surprised. According to her I look too big, too rough and too rude to be able to sing like that. But that's fine by me.

I never want anybody to think I'm boring or normal or ordinary, like them. I can make things happen in my life. I'm going to be famous. Everyone at school knows about the band and some kids stop and talk to me in the corridor, asking me how it's going, and wanting to know how to get tickets for the gig. The other day a lad in the lower-sixth even shouted, 'Hey, Will. Are you Happy?' And I replied, 'Yeah. I hope you are too!' It was really funny. It's amazing, but I've never noticed before how many people there actually are who wish they were in a band.

Thinking about it, being in this music shop now kind of proved how different I was to most people. We were supposed to be in lessons this afternoon; I was supposed to be in economics with Mr Adams. All of those other kids my age were sitting in a cramped classroom working on their marginal utilities and diminishing returns. And here I was, working on making my dreams come true.

I finished the song and handed the guitar back to my friend. 'Danny,' I said, 'you *need* this guitar.'

'Are you sure *you* don't want it?' he asked.

I didn't understand. 'There's nothing wrong with my guitar,' I told him.

But he ignored me, his face immediately brightening up once he'd slipped the strap round his shoulder again. 'What d'you think, Beth?' he asked.

She shrugged. 'It does look nice,' she admitted. 'It's a bit expensive, though.'

Danny looked at the tag, wincing sightly. 'Yeah,' he said. 'It'd take me ages to pay it off.'

'But think of how cool you'll look at Swift's,' I told him. 'Imagine what it'd look like with the lights reflecting on it.'

He was smiling again, nodding. 'Yeah.'

The owner returned with a little practice amp.

'How much deposit would you want for this?' I asked him.

The big guy made a thoughtful face, then blew out a loud breath as if deciding against his better judgement to do us a favour.

'Hundred,' he said.

Danny winced again, turning to me, disappointment on his face.

'Just don't get your mum that rug,' I said.

But Danny shrugged. He looked at the price tag again. He touched the guitar's strings, ran his fingers along the neck. He looked at both Beth and me, wanting us to persuade him.

Beth said, 'There's loads of others to choose from, Danny.'

But I knew that that was no help. He'd already fallen in love with this one.

'Your mum might not even want a rug,' I said. 'And even if you do buy her one, she might not put it in the living room. What happens if she wants it in the hall?'

Danny was staring at the price tag almost as if he could lower it by force of will.

'It just depends on how much the band means to you,' I told him.

Beth tutted at me. But Danny nodded. He understood.

'I'll take it,' he said.

THE CHASE

I'd forgotten about Richard Fitch. If I'd stopped for a minute to think things over, then I would have realised instantly that he certainly wasn't going to forget us. But everything had been moving so fast recently; the night at the scout hut seemed so long ago . . . I should have guessed that he wasn't going to let me steal his prize possession without a fight so I shouldn't have been at all surprised when he finally caught up with us.

'Oi, Ginger!'

Gavin, Danny and I were just leaving school after another boring day away from our music. Ian was picking us up at the gates for an extra-long rehearsal I'd arranged, seeing as we only had a month to go now before the gig. Looking forward to a whole night of playing had made the day bearable. Just.

'Hey, Gav!'

Neither me nor Danny recognised him at first. His hair had grown quite a bit since the last time we'd seen him, and the dye had all been washed out. It took a couple of seconds for me to cotton on. And then I kicked myself for not realising sooner. Gav knew exactly who it was, however. He swore, and made as if to walk away in the opposite direction. But Fitch already had a hand on his shoulder.

'How're you doing, Ginge? Long time no see.' He'd followed us across the teachers' car park. He was a wiry, spiteful-looking kid, wearing a pair of tight, faded jeans and a heavy, padded jacket, which gave his top half the appearance of being unnaturally wide compared to the rest of him. He smiled without showing any of his teeth and patted Gavin on the back. He didn't acknowledge me or Danny.

'Been looking for you,' he said, putting his arm round Gavin's shoulders and holding him close enough for it to be an embrace. 'I've managed to get us a gig at Christmas, and I can't do it without the best drummer in town, can I, eh? So what d'you reckon? You up for it?'

Gavin outweighed Fitch by a good two to three stone, but when he glanced quickly at me and Danny, he looked as nervous as hell.

He shrugged. 'I'm . . . I'm, you know. I'm wuh-with another b-b-band now,' he said.

But Fitch shook his head and hugged the drummer even closer. 'No, you're not.' He smiled. 'You'll always be one of us.' He winked.

A car horn honked, and we had to step out of the way for Mr Hogarth and his Volvo estate to get by. Danny and I moved one way, Fitch took Gavin the other. 'I can highly recommend the use of footpaths,' the history teacher said, staring straight at me as he drove past. But I didn't take any notice. I was too worried about what Fitch was saying to our drummer. He had his hand on Gavin's arm and was trying to lead him away.

I didn't get too close. 'Leave him alone, Fitch.'

But he didn't look at me. 'Tell your mate to shut his face,' he said calmly to Gavin, 'or I'll shut it for him.' He was still smiling his thin, close-lipped smile.

Gavin squirmed. Danny came to stand next to me and I hoped that maybe the fact that there were two of us would pressure Fitch into standing down.

'What's your problem?' I asked. 'We've got no grief with you.'

I could understand why he wanted Gavin back badly enough to cause a conflict. Putting aside the fact that it made him look bad having his drummer stolen, and not forgetting how brilliant Gav could be behind a kit, the problem was that drummers were so few and far between. Everyone you met wanted to be the singer, or the guitarist, because they were always the most famous ones. Drummers very rarely attained the same cult status. And there's even the old joke: What do you call someone who hangs around with a bunch of musicians? A drummer.

I'm not saying it's right or fair, it's just the way it is. That, added to the fact that few who had the desire also had the cash for a decent kit, or had a spare room big enough to store it, or parents willing to put up with the noise, obviously made them something akin to gold dust. So it was no wonder Fitch was here. And there was no chance I was going to step aside and let him have his way.

But Fitch carried on ignoring me. 'I'm telling you, Ginge, this gig'll be great. The biggest we've done so far.'

I took a step closer. 'He doesn't play for you any more. He's in my band now.'

Fitch laughed; a short chuff of air.

'L-look, Rich . . .' Gavin mumbled.

At last Fitch let the drummer go. He turned squarely to face me. 'You stole him from me, and now I'm stealing him back. So get lost, Honey Monster.'

There was a small ripple of laughter from behind me and I suddenly realised we were attracting quite a crowd. Some of the other kids on their way home had noticed the four of us standing in the middle of the car park and could tell there was trouble brewing. Kids are good at that, they can smell a fight a mile off (compared to teachers, who always seem much slower on the uptake). The little crowd gathered at the edge of the path. I cringed inwardly at their laughter.

'Find yourself another drummer,' I said. My heart was beginning to thump in my chest. Fitch was still smiling at me; he'd probably never backed down from a fight in his life.

'Don't need to,' he smirked. He wanted me to have a go. And was ready for it. But I couldn't let him take my drummer. I could feel the shaky expectancy of adrenalin in my legs. 'Big kids don't scare me,' he said.

'Stupid ones don't scare me.'

My heart was pounding. But I couldn't let him belittle me in front of everybody. Not now. There was too much at stake. The crowd of kids seemed to be pushing me from behind, forcing me to make my move. There was an itching, tingling sensation in the palms of my hands.

Fitch put his arm back round Gavin's shoulders. 'Tell the yeti to drop dead, will you, Gav?' The crowd laughed again, and Fitch was on a roll. 'Or is it Bigfoot?' he asked me. 'Maybe even . . .'

But I was lunging at him before he'd had chance to finish . . .

He was turning instantly to meet me with his fists raised . . .

And a car horn was blaring before I'd had chance to land a blow . . .

A red Metro seemed to appear from out of nowhere, scattering the four of us in different directions. The crowd of kids instantly disappeared. The car screeched to a halt. Fitch had to jump backwards or he would have been knocked over by it. I was breathing heavily, clenching and unclenching my fists, never taking my eyes off him. I waited for whichever teacher it was driving to start giving me a rollicking.

'Cavalry's here,' Ian said. And poked his head out of the driver's side window.

I was as surprised as anyone, but I still refused to take my eyes off Fitch. Danny and Gavin were quick to bundle themselves into the back seat, however. They left the door open and hissed at me to follow them. But I just kept staring at Fitch. I wanted to fight him now, I wanted to grind him into the dirt. I wanted him to know he hadn't beaten me. I wanted him to know that he was a talentless joke, a loser; the opposite of me. I waited for him to call me something else, anything else. But he stayed quiet, simply glaring at me.

Danny and Gavin were looking frantic, waving madly at me to get in the car. I climbed slowly into the passenger seat, crushing myself up, feeling undignified and stupid, and hating Ian for owning a Metro. I realised Fitch must have thought Ian was a teacher too. He watched the four of us, his nasty, slitted eyes flicking between us.

'Let's go,' Danny said. 'Quick.'

Ian nodded, and revved the engine, but seemed to change his mind. He didn't pull away. He looked at Fitch and shook his head. 'What must your mother think?' he asked.

Fitch looked shocked by the remark. He took a step towards us. 'Are you talking to me?'

I wasn't sure what Ian was doing exactly, but I was more than willing to see Fitch humiliated in any way possible.

'I know who you are, young man,' Ian said, play-acting as a teacher. 'I'll be telling your mother all about your behaviour here today, don't think I won't.'

I heard Gavin mumble something fretful behind me, but Fitch looked confused. It made me laugh.

'You should be ashamed of yourself,' Ian told him. 'You're a disgrace.'

Fitch saw me laughing at him and came right up to the Metro, bending forward to lean in at the driver's window. 'What did you say?'

Ian was face to face with him. 'And I'll tell you something else, sonny,' he said. 'Even my dog's backside is better looking.' Then he popped him the finger and wheel-spinned the little Metro away so quickly he would have taken Fitch's head off if he'd been leaning any further inside the window.

He giggled like a loon and took the car at top speed out through the school gates. Kids scattered. A couple of girls on their bikes squealed, wobbled, and fell off. And I howled with laughter.

Danny and Gavin didn't seem to see the funny side, however.

'What the hell was that for?' Danny fumed.

Gavin was staring out through the Metro's back window. 'You shouldn't have done that, Ian,' he said. 'You r-really shouldn't have done that.'

'Forget him,' I told them, dismissing Fitch with a wave of my hand. 'The guy's a jerk.'

'You really shouldn't have done that,' Gavin repeated. 'D-do you know who that was?'

Ian nodded, serious all of a sudden. 'Yeah, I know who that was. That was the moron who bullied my little cousin so much the poor kid was terrified of walking to school by himself. If I thought Will could have won I would have stayed out of it and let the moron get his face caved in a little.'

I was offended. 'Hey! Of course I could've won. I'm almost twice his size . . .'

But Gavin repeated, 'You really shouldn't have done that.'

And then Ian swore, his eyes going wide behind his glasses in the reflection of the rear-view mirror.

Danny and I twisted round in our seats to stare out of the back window with Gavin. There was a battered and rusty white Escort coming quickly up the road behind us. Ian took a left, and only a few seconds later, the Escort did too. Richard Fitch was hunched in the driver's seat.

All four of us swore at once. Ian took a right, picking up speed. Then another. A left. And the Escort followed.

'What're we going to do?' Danny groaned.

'It's Gav he's after, right?' Ian said. 'Let's just dump him at the side of the road and run.'

Danny wasn't amused. 'God, Ian. This is no time to be messing around.'

'Who says I'm messing around?' the bassist replied.

He weaved the Metro in and out of the back streets around the comp, and the Escort matched him turn for turn. He was driving in circles but Fitch didn't seem to be getting bored. We turned right onto Bedford Street, left onto Maitland Road. Back onto Kelly Way and we drove by the school gates for the second time. The Escort kept gaining and falling back only to reappear a few seconds later.

'This is crazy,' Ian was saying. 'He's not going to stop until he runs out of petrol.'

'Or w-we do,' Gavin put in.

'He's your friend,' Danny said to him. 'If we stopped couldn't you talk to him?'

'We're not stopping,' I said. 'If he wants a chase, then that's what we're gonna give him.' Danny went to speak again, but I wouldn't let him. 'He doesn't scare me.' I turned to Ian. 'Get onto a main road,' I said. 'Lose him in the traffic.'

Let him chase us, I was thinking. He's a jerk. He reckons he's in *Starsky and Hutch* or something. It was laughable.

Ian dodged into the flow of traffic on Carvard Avenue and was at last able to get the Metro above forty miles per hour. The little red car rattled and shook around us as it sped along towards the roundabout on Trewavas Avenue.

'Why aren't there any seatbelts back here?' Danny asked nervously. But Ian just told him to shut up.

'He's still behind us,' Gavin said, and was promptly told the same.

There was too much traffic travelling in both directions for Ian to be able to overtake the car in front and put some distance between us and Fitch, too many parents picking up their children from school. He kept edging out into the centre of the road, but there was simply no opening for him to move into. Luckily there was a Fiesta directly behind us which Fitch had to get past before he could get to us. Unfortunately the old man in the flat cap who was driving didn't seem to realise what his accelerator pedal was for. So as we sped on, and he fell back, a gap large enough for an Escort was gradually forming.

'Watch it!' Danny shouted, leaping up from his seat in alarm.

Without warning a suicidal lollipop lady had stepped into the road. The Nissan in front of us showed its brake lights. Ian hit his own brakes so hard that Gavin was flung forward into the back of my seat. Even I cried out. And the Metro skidded to a halt.

The bloke driving the Nissan turned to look at us through his rear window. A troupe of young children crossed the road cautiously, watching us all the time, ready to run for it at the slightest hint of a revving engine, while the lollipop lady scowled. I think all four of us blushed, but at least the Escort-sized gap behind us had shrunk again.

Ian moved off extra carefully when the lollipop lady returned to the footpath and the four of us all looked away, ducking our heads so we didn't have to meet her stare.

'God, Ian . . .' Danny said, looking down at his lap, only giving the older lad a dirty glare when we were well out of sight of her.

'He's still coming,' Gavin needlessly informed us.

'Come on, Ian. Just pull over,' Danny said. 'Someone's going to have an accident.'

I nodded. 'Yeah. Fitch is. Keep going, Ian.'

I spotted a space which had miraculously appeared in the oncoming traffic. 'There,' I shouted, pointing at it. 'Go, go!'

Ian went for it, swerving the rattling, shaking Metro out into the opposite lane, leap-frogging the Nissan in front of us. And Fitch did the same to the Fiesta behind, keeping the distance between us to a single car. I laughed out loud. This really was *Starsky and Hutch*!

We reached the roundabout. Ian slowed down, signalled to turn right onto Clee Hill Road, but realised too late that the Nissan behind was signalling left. He tried to change lanes to keep in front of it, to keep it between us and Fitch, and was assaulted by blaring horns from all sides. Then the Nissan was gone, and Fitch's Escort was right on our tail.

Ian's voice was too high-pitched by far. 'Where to? Where am I going?' He seemed to have lost his famous sense of humour. He circled the roundabout once, twice, three times. The four exits flashed by. Other drivers waiting patiently to use the roundabout watched our Metro and Fitch's Escort with bemused expressions. Danny and Gavin were thrown around on the back seat as if they were on a fairground ride.

I was watching over my shoulder for the gap. 'Not yet. Keep going.' I saw Fitch coming up right behind us. 'Wait for it.' Then: 'Left! Now! Left!'

More car horns, but this time aimed at Fitch as he tried to follow us at the last minute. Ian put the pedal to the metal, and the little Metro shot up Trewavas Avenue, leaving Fitch trapped to circle the roundabout one more time.

I laughed out loud again. 'We lost him.' No one else seemed to think it was funny.

There were fewer cars now. Trewavas Avenue headed towards the traffic lights at the top of Town Road, and from there on to Stonner, out of town. Ian was able to push his Metro for all it was worth, trying to get some extra distance between us and Fitch. We virtually flew down the road. We were all checking over our shoulders, but there was nothing behind us now. Ian wasn't taking any chances though, and kept his speed above sixty all the way up to the traffic lights. They changed to red and his little car shuddered to a halt.

'I can't see him.'

'We've lost him.'

'He's probably still on the roundabout.'

'Maybe . . .'

We saw the Escort come hurtling over the rise in the road. We turned like synchronised swimmers to look at the red light glaring down on us. Then, with precision timing, back to the white Escort.

'Go, Ian,' I said.

He shook his head. 'I can't. It's red.'

Fitch wasn't slowing down.

'He's not s-s-slowing down,' Gavin said.

I began to feel nervous for the first time. 'Come on, Ian. Just go.'

He still shook his head. 'There might be something coming.' He leaned forward, trying to see past the trees on the corner.

Fitch still wasn't slowing down.

Danny said, 'He's going to ram us.'

And I said, 'Don't be stupid.' Then, 'Go now, Ian. Come on.'

'But . . .'

'It's still red,' Gavin said.

'Ian . . .'

'I can't . . .'

'He's not slowing down.'

'Oh, God!'

'Ian . . .'

'But . . .'

'Jesus Christ, Ian!'

The little Metro lurched away from the red light, making Gavin yelp and me grip my seat. I heard a car horn. It was Ian trying to warn anything coming the other way. We shot across the junction. It felt as though we'd kangarooed the road in a single bound. And something *was* coming – the 3C bus bound for Stonner and the villages beyond. I saw the look in the driver's eyes. But we missed it by a good distance. It was touch and go whether Fitch would . . .

The sound of the double-decker's horn was much louder than ours. All four of us turned fully round to look, even Ian, as he pulled up sharply at the side of the road. The bus obscured most of our view, but we saw the white Escort swerve dangerously. There were passengers leaping to their feet, flinging their arms above their heads in mute panic. We heard tyres squeal. We heard the crash. Only when the bus moved unharmed out of the way did we see Fitch's car bounced up onto the pavement with its front end crumpled up and wrapped around the traffic light. It was still on red.

Danny and Gavin both swore. Ian looked frightened.

The 3C's driver and a couple of male passengers jumped out of the bus and ran over to the Escort. Fitch climbed unsteadily out of the wreck. He let two of the men hold him upright for a moment. Then he was sick.

The four of us watched the scene in silence. Ian was white and shaking slightly.

'Let's go,' I said to him.

'Shouldn't we help?' he asked.

But I just shook my head. We'd only get involved and have a hell of a lot of explaining to do.

'We can't just leave him,' Danny said.

'You stay then,' I told him. 'You stay. I'm not.' The three of them all looked at me as if I was an alien and we'd been flying in my spaceship for the last ten minutes. I shrugged at them. 'Serves him right for messing with the band.'

No one spoke as Ian put the car into gear and drove slowly away. I put a tape in the stereo and sat back. I wasn't worried. I'd won.

BAD NEWS X 2

The accident made page four in the local newspaper, which I reckoned only went to prove what I'd believed all along: Richard Fitch would never be worthy of making the front page. I guess it was lucky we hadn't been implicated. There was no mention of a little red Metro at the scene whatsoever, and I know Ian was able to sleep better at night because of it, but it soon seemed as though it was the last piece of good fortune we were going to get. With only two weeks left before the gig things suddenly started going wrong. And it was especially galling to think we'd maybe wasted that luck thanks to Fitch.

First of all, Danny's mum saw the stain.

It was a Tuesday night, a rehearsal night, and Gavin, Ian and I were hanging around outside the flower shop's back door waiting for Danny to arrive with the keys to let us in.

'Maybe we should give him a ring,' Gavin said.

Ian nodded. 'He might need a lift.'

It was a cold, blustery night and the three of us were squeezed in the back of the hire van Gavin's dad always used to ferry our gear around. I had a cymbal stand poking painfully into the small of my back. Danny had told me earlier that he'd meet us here. He'd said he was coming with his dad, because there was something he wanted to pick up from the shop, but he should still have been here by now. I was tutting and sighing, getting more and more annoyed as the minutes passed.

'What time is it?' I asked.

'Ten past,' Ian told me.

We were wasting valuable rehearsal time. Didn't he realise we only had a couple of weeks to go?

'I'm thinking of buying a cheap van actually,' Gavin's dad shouted over his shoulder from the front seat. 'It's costing me an arm and a leg to keep hiring this one out twice a week. I just need to persuade Gavin's mum, is all, 'cos it's the money for her Christmas present I'll be spending.'

At least this raised a smile, even though I knew he was probably dead serious. He was great, Mr Fisher – he seemed to really care about the band, and was always putting himself out for us. Most parents would have told their kids to get their heads out of the clouds and concentrate on their education first. But not Gavin's dad; he actively encouraged his son to play his drums. Danny said it was probably because he would have loved the chance to do something special when he was younger, and was using Gavin to fulfil his own ambitions. But I just reckoned it was because he had his head screwed on right. He was the complete opposite of Danny's dad. I mean, he already had a van for his shop's delivery service, but not once had he offered to shift our gear in it.

'Maybe if you put some tinsel round the steering wheel, you could say it *was* her Christmas present?' Ian offered.

Mr Fisher laughed. And that was when Danny decided to show up. He looked really miserable. Mr Graham didn't look very happy either to tell the truth. I realised something must be wrong then. Danny was walking with a slouch, like he was at a funeral, and I noticed immediately that he wasn't carrying his guitar. His dad unlocked the back door.

We all jumped out of the van. 'Where've you been? Where's your guitar?' I asked.

'We've got a problem,' Danny said quietly. But he wouldn't say any more until his dad had disappeared inside the shop. Gavin and Ian already had bits of the drum kit between them and were heading for the shop door. Mr Fisher was carrying my amp. 'We're not allowed to use the back room any more. My mum's gone crazy.'

We all gathered round, knowing from his whisper that he didn't want his dad to hear.

'What d'you mean?' I asked. 'What's happened?'

'She noticed the stain, didn't she? From the night with the beer. She went absolutely mental.'

'But that's weeks old,' Ian said.

Gavin didn't say anything; he just looked a bit anxious with his own dad being there.

I couldn't quite get my head round it. 'So she's said we can't rehearse in the shop because of it?'

Danny nodded glumly.

'That's ridiculous. How'd she know it was your fault?'

'Well I had to tell her, didn't I?'

I shook my head incredulously. What a stupid question. 'No. You didn't have to tell her a thing.'

'Oh, come on, Will . . .'

'What d'you mean, "Oh, come on"? I bet you blabbed the whole thing, didn't you?'

He shrugged, and I could have hit him. He was such a wimp sometimes, he never stuck up for himself. And now he'd lost us our rehearsal room.

Ian said, 'Oh, God. Now I'm in trouble too.'

Danny mumbled some sort of an apology, but I was fuming.

'Don't you realise we've only got two weeks to go?' I

shouted at him. 'Doesn't it matter to you that we need to rehearse here? I can't believe you told her what happened. What are you? Stupid or something? You know what a miserable cow your mum is!'

And with that his dad came storming out of the shop.

'Don't you dare talk about my wife like that, young man! I think it's been very good of her to let you use the shop for so long, don't you? And in my opinion she's perfectly right to punish you all for ruining a five-hundred-pound carpet. If I were you I'd be thanking my lucky stars she's not asking me to replace it.'

But I was too angry to reply. I simply glared at him. Compared to my dad, and Gavin's, he was a jerk. I grabbed my guitar from the back of the hire van and walked away.

Of course, by the time I got home Danny's mum had been on the phone to my house, kicking up a stink. My grandma made me call back and say I was sorry, which I did once I'd cooled off a little. I was beginning to feel more worried than angry anyway. We really needed that back room. Where were we supposed to rehearse now? Didn't *anybody* realise we only had two weeks to go?

But the worst was yet to come.

The following morning I'd managed to calm down. I decided it would be better if I apologised to everyone, so when I got to school I made a point of finding Danny before he disappeared to his first lesson. It's weird, but I didn't like the thought of having him mad at me. I could stand his sister not liking me, and his parents thinking I was rude, but he was my oldest friend, and I knew I'd gone well over the top with what I'd said to him the night before. If I wanted anybody to be on my side, if I wanted anybody standing right there next to me in the spotlight, then it had to be Danny.

For as long as I could remember we'd always planned to do things together, we'd always had shared ambitions. When we were in the junior school we'd told everybody we were going to travel the world together. As soon as we could leave home and not have to listen to our parents any more we were going to throw a backpack over our shoulders and wander off for as long as five or six years. We bought ourselves an atlas and decided on which countries to visit and for how long. We even wrote exactly the same Christmas list one year, asking for hiking boots, sleeping bags and a compass each. We kept that particular dream alive until we moved up to the comp, but then it sort of faded and I can't really remember why. I guess you just find new things to dream about as you get older.

But we had loads of different schemes and ideas; we were always planning on doing something together. Unfortunately, none of them had really got any further than the insides of our heads so far. Which was what made Happy all the more special. This idea seemed to be working. This dream seemed to be coming true.

I cornered him in the cloakroom as soon as he arrived. It was raining outside and I didn't even give him chance to get his wet coat off. I tried to make a bit of a joke out of it, telling him I knew exactly what kind of a pillock I was, and explaining once again how important this gig and Happy were to me. And luckily, Danny being Danny, he understood. He forgave me with a shrug . . . Then told me the bad news.

'We didn't know what to do after you went,' he said. 'Ian said we ought to go see the guy at Swift's, just to make sure that he'd listened to the tape and that everything was still okay with us playing there . . .'

I could feel it coming. 'Don't tell me he hated the tape. He must have liked it. It took us ages to do.'

But Danny shook his head. 'No, no. He thought we sounded great. He was really impressed.'

'I don't get it,' I said. 'What's wrong then?'

Danny didn't want to say. He looked kind of shifty, nervous. I guessed I couldn't blame him after my outburst last night. So I promised myself I wouldn't explode again. I told myself that whatever the problem was we could work it out. Maybe we had to pay to play there? I'd heard bands had to do that sometimes. Or maybe he was changing the date until after Christmas? Which would be disappointing admittedly, but not disastrous.

'It's because we're only seventeen,' he said.

But I still didn't click on. 'Yeah? And?'

'He says he can't let minors into his nightclub.'

'You what?'

'He says we're not old enough to play there.'

I was stunned into silence. I quite literally couldn't think of anything to say. We'd lost our gig . . . We weren't allowed to play any more . . .

Danny was quickly trying to explain. 'We told him that Ian was twenty-one, but he didn't want to listen. He said he could get into trouble if we played there. He said he wouldn't let us play until we were all eighteen, or he'd get done by the police . . .'

I found my voice again. 'That's rubbish!' I shouted. 'That's a lie!'

'We were arguing with him for ages. Ian got really angry. Even Gav's dad tried to sort it out for us.'

I wanted to explode. I wanted to go crazy. But I knew it wasn't Danny's fault. Everything seemed to be falling apart. I ranted and raved at him, yet it was the manager of Swift's I was swearing and shouting about. I couldn't believe what was happening. After everything we'd done. After all our hard work. I was giving up everything for this band and now we didn't have anywhere to rehearse or anywhere to play. In the space of two days we'd lost everything.

I stared at Danny. His wet coat steamed gently in the warm air of the cloakroom. 'My father was supposed to be coming to watch me,' I said.

Two Songs

I was only fifteen, maybe twenty minutes late getting to the cinema, and Beth had already gone. I'd spent all day running around like a headless chicken, desperately trying to get things sorted, and I wasn't really in the mood to have an argument with my girlfriend on top. I felt like going home straight away, but guessed I'd better look for her. So I checked in the foyer, and even nipped across the road to the café where we'd sometimes had a drink on previous nights out together, but the place was empty. I couldn't find her anywhere. I wasn't sure if she might have gone to watch the film by herself, and hung around outside wondering whether or not to risk it and go in, just in case she had. In the end, though, I decided I'd had enough and caught the bus home. It wasn't really my type of film. And the soundtrack was rubbish anyway.

She was waiting for me when I got back. She was sitting having a cup of coffee with my grandparents in the living room. Grandma and Grandad both seemed to be a bit upset with me, but Beth looked madder than hell.

We went upstairs to my room.

'So? Where were you? No, let me guess. At Danny's.'

'Yeah, look, Beth, I'm really sorry I was late . . .'

'And what were you doing? Oh, I wonder. Could it be something to do with Happy perhaps?' She was almost spitting froth she was so angry. Her eyes blazed.

I sat on the floor but Beth didn't take up her usual position on the edge of my bed. She paced up and down the room instead. She was wearing a denim miniskirt with dark tights underneath which made her long legs look twice the length, sleek, and very sexy. She was wearing a new cropped jacket I'd never seen before with a white T-shirt underneath. I think she'd even had her hair cut, and was wearing her favourite hairslide, all glittery and blue. And it was maybe only the third or fourth time I'd ever seen her in make-up. She looked stunning. I wanted to tell her so, but didn't have the guts.

'Do you know how cold I got standing there waiting for you dressed like this? All these people giving me funny looks, thinking I must be crazy in this weather. And I guess I am crazy. Yeah, real crazy. Stupid, a moron! Because I did it all for you.'

'I really am sorry, Beth,' I said, reaching for my guitar, simply through force of habit. 'It's just . . .'

'Put that down!' she shrieked. 'Put it down or I'm leaving right now!'

I nearly dropped the thing in shock. I looked up at her.

'I mean it, Will. Just for once, leave your stupid guitar alone and give *me* some attention instead.'

I moved very slowly, unsure of what she would do next, not willing to take any risks. It crossed my mind that maybe she really had gone crazy.

She watched me put my guitar back on its stand then knelt on the floor in front of me. She spoke very quietly now, almost in a whisper. 'Do you still like me?' she asked.

I nodded.

'Do you still like me enough to want to go out with me?'

I nodded again.

'Do you still find me attractive?'

'Of course I do.'

'So why do you keep treating me like dirt?' she screamed and slapped me across the face.

She was crying, but I was the one in pain. My cheek was killing me. And to tell the truth I had kind of been hoping for some sympathy from her. A kiss and a cuddle maybe while I told her how badly things were suddenly going for me and the band. Didn't she understand what was happening? It didn't even feel as if we had a band any more. We'd already missed two rehearsals this week, not that we had anything to rehearse for. I was miserable enough without Beth giving me any more grief.

She waited for me to say something, watching my eyes, but I simply didn't know what I could say. And eventually she got up to leave.

But I knew I didn't want her to leave. I was desperate for some comfort. She was my girlfriend, she was beautiful, I wanted her to stay.

'Beth,' I managed. 'Please. Don't go.'

She hovered in the doorway with her back to me. I'd had plenty of girlfriends in the past, but none of them had been anywhere near as good-looking as Beth. Everyone knew she was the prettiest girl at the comp. I couldn't let her leave. Everyone knew she was *my* girlfriend.

'We'll go to the pictures tomorrow,' I said. But she wouldn't turn round. 'I think you look really nice,' I told her. 'I like your jacket. Is it new?'

Even with her back to me I knew she was still crying.

'Things are going really badly with the band,' I tried to explain. 'We've lost our gig at Swift's, and Danny's mum won't let us use her shop to rehearse in any more.' I got up and walked over to her. I put my arms around her waist and kissed the back of her neck. 'We've spent all day trying to sort things out, we haven't even been in to school.'

She nodded. 'I know. Mr Holloway's been looking for you. He asked me where you were.'

Mr Holloway was the head of the sixth form. And a miserable old git who certainly wouldn't understand about the band.

'What did you tell him?'

'I just said I didn't know. But my dad told me at tea that all the teachers are talking about you.'

'Yeah? What are they saying?'

She shrugged. 'They're complaining that your homework never gets handed in on time any more, and that your grades are slipping. My dad reckons that you're going to have to work really hard if you want to get away to university next year. You're going to have to do really well in the mocks after Christmas.'

I tutted. 'Is that all anybody talks about any more? University?'

She was surprised by my tone of voice, and at last turned round to face me. 'What do you mean?'

I moved her over to the bed and we sat down next to each other.

'I just don't think I'm really bothered about it any more. I'm fed up with everyone going on about it all the time as if it's the be-all and end-all of life.'

Beth wasn't really crazy. Or stupid. 'Because the band's more important?'

I nodded.

'That's ridiculous. You can't throw everything away just because you've learned how to play the guitar.'

'But that's what I want to do. I want to write songs and play in a band. What's wrong with that?'

She sighed at me. 'You've got your head too high in the clouds.'

'So?' I slid off the bed and searched through the pile of CDs on my floor.

'So . . . So everything. You can't just give up your A levels and become a rock star.'

I found the album I was after and put it into the player. I turned the volume up loud. 'Listen,' I told her.

The guitars started slow, drifting, winding in and out of each other. The drums gave them a focus, and they followed the beat for a time, then lifted above it, spiralling up and up and up, until . . . You couldn't make out the singer's every word, but you knew exactly how he felt. His voice flowed like the guitars, it carried you along, it made you understand the pain he was feeling.

He sang:

'I believe in returns and in boomerangs,
In the rush of the ground as you release my hand,
The attraction to earth of these fragile bones,
Will hurt much more than their sticks and stones.'

And listening to him made you realise how much you were hurting too, because he was singing about a pain you also had somewhere inside, somewhere deep and hidden. He was somehow tapping into the emotions that everybody has, but would never be able to express without his music. It was like this guy knew exactly who you were, knew precisely how you felt and wished he could help, but was suffering just the same.

When it finished I turned the stereo off and looked at Beth. 'See what songs can do?' I asked. And I could tell she knew exactly what I was talking about.

'I've got goosebumps,' she said with a little laugh.

'Exactly. That's *exactly* what I mean. A levels can't do that, they can't make you feel things. But I want to write songs that do.'

She didn't know what to say now. She was a teacher's daughter, she'd had it drummed into her all her life that it was education, education, education that mattered most. And she believed it, which was fine. I was different. My father had taught me something else.

'I just wish . . .' she began, but faltered.

'What?' I asked.

She shook her head.

'No, please, tell me.'

She sighed. 'I don't know, I just wish you'd talk to me sometimes.'

'I do talk to you.'

'But only ever about music. You hear a song on TV and you tell me who wrote it, and if it's any good, and why you don't like it, and which other song is better. And the other day you wouldn't go clothes shopping with me because—'

'I did go shopping with you!'

'But you refused to go into that shop just because you didn't like the music they were playing.'

'I can't help thinking Michael Jackson's a jerk. I'm not the only one, you know.'

Beth flung up her hands in exasperation. 'It's taken over your life, Will. Can't you see that?'

I didn't say a word. I looked at my stereo.

'What if you don't make it?' she asked eventually. 'Hundreds of people want to be in a band. They all get guitars and they all play gigs and they all write songs, and they still never make it.'

'But they're not me.'

She shrugged, then came and knelt beside me again. 'I

hope you're right,' she said. 'I mean that.' She kissed my lips. 'I really do.'

I grinned at her to let her know it wasn't a problem. 'I've started writing a new song,' I told her. 'Do you want to hear it?'

She smiled and nodded.

'Not quite as good as that last one,' I said, grabbing my guitar and plugging in. 'And Gav says it's too slow. But he's a drummer, he says everything's too slow.' I was trying to make her smile.

I found the opening chord and cleared my throat.

I sang:

'Still down, still blue,
Too old to be sniffing glue,
Need a different fix,
Another high on something new,
That's why I'm still here waiting for you . . .'

But by the time I'd finished, she'd gone.

Dumping 'Dirty Dancing'

I felt like I'd been run over. Over and over. I'd never felt so low before. I had to sort myself out.

Everything seemed to be slipping away from me. I was letting people down. My grandparents expected me to work hard at school. Beth expected me to be a sensitive, caring boyfriend, and Danny, Gavin and Ian expected me to have everything to do with the band under control. But over the past few days I'd somehow lost my grip on it all. I couldn't do anything right. I didn't know what to do for the best. I was stuck.

Again I skipped school. I did it properly this time, however, and feigned illness in front of my grandma, so at least I was assured a sick note to hand in. I just needed an extra day to tidy my thoughts up a bit, to get things straight. And I spent the full day alone in my room exhaustively combing through my CD collection, disc by disc.

I guess you could say I was deciding exactly what kind of person I wanted to be. I was subtracting anything I didn't feel properly fitted with how I saw myself. And anything that didn't suit this ideal was, quite simply, removed.

To be honest, I'd been doing this for years already anyway. Music was something I'd talked a lot about at school, even before Happy, and the size of my CD collection was well known. Some people I talked to would ask me which one had been the first I'd ever bought, and my answer has always been

Sound Affects by the Jam, even though it's a complete lie. That particular CD was in fact the third I'd bought. But who can blame me for not wanting to talk about the *Dirty Dancing* soundtrack, volumes one and two, being the honest to goodness truth? I saw the film at an early and, I suppose, impressionable age, and I bought the two CDs with birthday money when I was eight. I sincerely believe that any music purchases before the age of ten shouldn't count – you're just too naive to know what good music is when you're so young. I actually bought the Jam album when I was thirteen, when my father gave me my first stereo and I didn't have to use my grandparents' machine any more. I only bought it because the nice guy with glasses working at Virgin recommended it to me, and it was on sale. The band themselves had split up years before (the album was actually a year older than me; I felt I had so much catching up to do), and yet their music was the first I'd ever heard that made me want to do more than just tap my feet. It was so full of energy. It was fantastic and furious.

The problem was, I still had those two *Dirty Dancing* CDs. I'd never got rid of them before because they filled my collection out, but they were definitely embarrassing. I think you can discover what kind of a person you're dealing with by first ferreting through his CDs, and what did those particular two say about me, about who I was? So I spent the day being ruthless.

I picked carefully through my collection, weeding out anything which I felt did not suit Will Brown, singer, guitarist, song-writer. And I didn't just put them in a box to hide away in the bottom of my wardrobe, I binned them. I pulled the cases apart, tore up the booklets, and snapped the shiny discs in half. I spent the day re-shaping my taste in music, and therefore re-shaping me. I was erasing mistakes from my past.

I was left a stripped, thinner person, but definitely more thoughtful, more discerning.

I got a lot of thinking done that day, about what everybody expected of me, about what was happening with Beth and school and the band. And I began to wonder exactly what my father's expectations were. He was the only person I could think of who had never really told me what he wanted me to do, or be. Except once. One time, when I'd been about thirteen or fourteen, he'd been home for Christmas and he'd said that all he ever wanted for me to be was happy. That was all. Nothing else. Just happy.

I thought about it hard, looking at my new CD collection, feeling better about myself already. And that was when things fell back into place. It suddenly dawned on me that maybe all was not lost after all. I remembered what had happened with Richard Fitch a couple of weeks ago, and realised that with a bit of luck maybe we could get ourselves a gig after all.

I called an urgent meeting, seven o'clock sharp. The four of us crowded into my bedroom, and Ian was the first to notice the difference.

'What's happened to your CDs?' he asked.

'I've had a bit of a sort out,' I told him. 'I wanted to get rid of some of the rubbish.'

Danny was the most shocked. 'There's loads missing,' he said. 'What've you done with them all?'

'I've dumped them.'

'What? Thrown them out? What for?'

'They made me look like I didn't know what decent music was.'

'They couldn't have all been that bad.' He was searching through what was left. 'You've still got those two Elton John albums,' he sneered. 'They would've been the first to go from *my* collection.'

Gavin and Ian laughed as well, and I just tried to shrug it off. Danny always picked on those two CDs. He thought it was clever trying to embarrass me in public by telling people about them. And there was no way I was going to tell him they'd been a present from my father.

'Have you chucked them all?' Gavin asked, also searching to see what was missing.

I nodded. 'Yeah. I got rid of about twenty-five or so, I think. No longer will I be seen as the sort of person suckered into buying the new Levellers album simply because they were almost quite good once.' And I looked at Danny because I knew full well he had just bought it.

The three of them continued to pore over my revitalised collection for a few minutes more, tutting and shaking their heads in disbelief at what I'd done. ('Twenty-five?' Ian whispered. 'That's getting on for about three hundred and fifty quid he's just thrown away.') Then I said, 'So, do you want to hear my good news, or what?'

'I could do with some,' Ian admitted. But he didn't tell us why.

'And me,' Gavin said. 'Mr Holloway had me and Danny in his office half the afternoon, didn't he, Danny? He was going ape.'

Danny nodded and rolled his eyes. 'Lucky you weren't there,' he told me. 'Somebody's noticed about us skipping lessons recently and told him. I was dead worried he was going to tell my mum, because you know what she'd be like. Holloway's bad enough, but he's nowhere near as scary as she is.'

We all laughed, except for Ian, who didn't seem very cheerful at all. I wondered whether or not he'd had his confrontation with Mrs Graham about the stained carpet yet. Or whether it was something worse that was playing on his mind. Maybe he and Danny's sister were having problems?

'He's after you too, Will,' Gavin said. 'He says some of the other teachers have been complaining about you.'

'Yeah, I know. Beth told me.'

'He reckons we've got to have any outstanding assignments handed in by next week,' Danny said. 'Or he's going to get *personally* involved with our lessons.'

'What's that mean?' I asked.

But both Danny and Gavin shrugged. Getting bawled out by the teacher had clearly been a far from pleasant experience, and I immediately started calculating how difficult it would be for me to avoid the man for the rest of the term. We only had two weeks to go now before the Christmas holidays, so maybe it wouldn't be impossible . . .

I turned to Gavin. 'Do you know Fitch's telephone number?' I asked him. He was a bit surprised by the question, but nodded all the same.

'What's he got to do with it?' Danny asked, already looking anxious.

I smiled my best smile, and opened my arms wide as if presenting them with a gift. 'He's going to get us a gig.'

They all started talking at once. 'What do you mean? How? Fitch hates us. He'd never do anything like that.'

I held up my hands to quieten them. 'Can you remember when he tried to get Gav back? He was really desperate for a drummer.'

Gavin just looked confused. 'Yeah. And?'

'He was desperate because he said Shoot Cliff had a gig lined up for Christmas.'

Danny wasn't getting it either. 'So?'

'So, maybe he hasn't been able to find one yet,' I said.

Ian smiled slowly as he twigged on. 'If he hasn't got a drummer, then he hasn't got a band, right?'

I nodded. 'Right.'

'And if he hasn't got a band, then he can't play the gig.'

I laughed. 'Exactly. But we could. All we need to do is find out where and when, then offer our services.'

Gavin was laughing right along with me. 'You're a genius, Will.' He slapped me on the back. 'Why didn't I think of that?' But I was in too good a mood to tell him.

'It's risky,' I admitted. 'Fitch might not want to talk, and it might be too late anyway . . .' But the three of them weren't listening. All their worries had instantly melted away. Danny hopped around the room singing, 'We've got a gig. We've got a gig. We've got a gig.'

We hustled Gavin downstairs to use the phone. He seemed nervous, but the prospect of getting to play in front of an audience again spurred him on. He had his little black book in his coat pocket and, buried somewhere in between dozens of girls' telephone numbers, he found Fitch's. Danny, Ian and I bunched up around him at the hall table, trying to hear what was said.

'Pretend you're interested in joining his band again,' I whispered into the drummer's ear. 'Just get him to tell you where the gig is.'

Gavin nodded quickly, then hushed us as the phone started ringing. We closed in tighter around him, straining to hear. It took ages for someone to answer, and then another few minutes for Fitch to come to the phone. Gavin was looking quite pale, but I knew he'd do it for the good of the band. I was willing him on, gripping his shoulder.

'Er, hiya Fitch, it's Guh-Guh-Gav.' He paused then asked, 'How's your c-c-car? . . . That bad, yeah? . . . Yeah, I'm really s-sorry.' He turned to look at me. 'No, no. I d-don't see him any more . . . Yeah. I'll tell him if I s-s-see him.' He drew a line across his neck with his finger to let me know exactly what Fitch wanted to do to me.

'Ssso, anyway. H-how's the band doing?' Danny, Ian and I were crushing up against him, desperate to hear what was being said on the other end of the phone. 'Yeah . . . Yeah . . . Oh, right.' I saw Danny had his fingers crossed. 'Wuh-where is it, d-did you say?' The four of us couldn't have had our faces closer together if we'd tried. 'Yeah . . . Yeah.' Then Gavin grinned and gave us the thumbs up. 'What day's that, then?' And Danny, Ian and I were leaping in silent joy around the hallway. 'O-okay,' Gav was saying. 'Yeah, okay. I'll think about it. I'll give you a ring if I can make it.' And he hung up quickly.

'Where is it?' I asked the instant he'd put the phone down. 'Where's the gig?'

Gavin was grinning like a hero. 'He said it's the Christmas disco at Stonner Secondary School, a week on Monday.'

I frowned a little, thinking that getting to play there could be a problem.

But Ian seemed even more enthusiastic. 'Stonner Secondary? That's great, it's my old school.' He was smiling more broadly than any of us now. 'We'll get the gig for sure. The teachers all love me there.'

We all cheered. Then Danny said, 'We still need somewhere to rehearse though.'

'We might be able to use my dad's garage,' Gavin told us.

'Why didn't you tell us that before?' Danny asked.

'Because we'd have to clear all the junk out of it first. It's full of old bikes and lawnmowers, and a washing machine and stuff. It'll take ages.'

'Doesn't matter,' I said, shaking my head to prove it. 'We can all do it together, no worries. Even if it takes us all day we'll still have somewhere to rehearse that night.'

We all cheered.

'Okay,' I said. 'This is the plan. Ian, you sweet-talk your old teachers and get us confirmed to play. Take them one of the tapes we made. Tell them how wonderful we are. Give them all of your money. Anything, okay?' He winked at me, letting me know it wasn't a problem.

'Gav, Danny, us three will work our backsides off over the weekend to do whatever homework we have to so Holloway can't hassle us any more, agreed?' They both nodded. 'All four of us will get together first thing Sunday morning to clear Mr Fisher's garage. Then we'll have a full week of rehearsals, meeting every night.' I paused for effect. 'And then the following Monday . . .'

And we all cheered again.

I felt great. I felt back on top again, right where I belonged.

The Gig

It was cold in the medical room, and dark; we'd pulled the blind down when some ugly year nine kid had pushed his spotty face up against the outside of the window. There was the faint smell of disinfectant in the air and the music from the main hall was numbed by the clean blue and white tiles on the walls. Ian had told us that, unlike the comp, Stonner Secondary didn't have a greenroom, and every Christmas, to the nurse's distress, her office was always crammed full of pupils in fancy dress waiting for their cue. We'd commandeered the small, cramped room for our own purposes tonight, however, because tonight was *our* night.

I had a heavy pain in my belly which felt something like a lead fart. I paced up and down the middle of the little room to try to ease it. I'd left my guitar set up on the stage and wished I had it with me, if only to keep my hands occupied. We were all nervous, but excited too. I don't think any of us had slept particularly well last night. Even though this wasn't our school they'd still allowed us to buy tickets for our friends and family, and they were packed into the hall along with all the Stonner kids. Every time the music faded from one record to the next we could hear their voices drifting down the corridor towards us.

Ian cradled his bass on the well-worn couch-cum-bed where he claimed he'd spent many a PE lesson. He plucked absently at the strings, not really playing anything, just trying to stop his fingers from shaking, I think. His glasses were in the top pocket of his shirt. He looked odd without them, younger. Gavin rattled his drumsticks against the nurse's desk, chair, windowsill, radiator, wastepaper bin, the noise irritating to everyone but himself. He bopped his cropped, ginger head and started singing. It made me glad he was the drummer. And Danny was crouched in the corner by the door chewing on a plectrum and tuning his guitar for at least the eighteenth time. It was his old one, battered and blue, with Tippex to mark the frets. He hadn't been able to afford the Gibson after paying to have his mum's carpet profession-ally cleaned, and had only just managed to get his deposit back after a long argument with the shop owner. He'd bought a new shirt especially for tonight; it was green and trendy, but already had dark patches underneath the arms.

He looked up from his guitar suddenly. 'Anyone got the time?' he asked.

Gavin wasn't listening and I shook my head.

So Ian pulled his glasses from out of his shirt pocket, unfolded the thick, black arms, then put them on his face before squinting down at his watch. And as he peered at it in the dim light I began to wonder if it had been such a wise move of ours to insist he didn't wear them on stage. We'd told him rock stars didn't wear specs.

'How long have we got?' Danny asked.

'About ten minutes,' Ian said.

Danny swore and anxiously hunkered down over his guitar again.

I watched Ian as he laboriously re-folded his glasses and put them back in his shirt pocket. 'Are you sure you're not going to need them on?' I asked him.

Ian grinned at me. 'I can see just fine,' he said, purposely staring a foot beyond my left shoulder.

'I'm not fooling about, Ian. I don't want you messing up. If you need . . .'

'Simmer down, Will. I'll be fine, okay?' He tutted and looked me dead in the eye. 'No worries.'

'I mean it.'

'I know you do,' Ian said. 'We *all* know you do.'

I shrugged. I wasn't exactly sure what he meant by that. I was going to ask, but Gavin suddenly stopped his drumming and pushed past me towards the door.

'I've got to go,' he said.

I grabbed his arm. Images of him legging it across the school's field sprang to mind, his ginger head bobbing out of sight.

'What do you mean? Where?'

He looked up at me, crinkling his face in a half-embarrassed, half-fearful kind of way. 'My s-stomach's going c-c-crazy,' he said. 'I swear I'll do it on s-s-stage if I duh-don't do it now.' He held a pale hand against his belly.

Ian started sniggering behind his bass, and I told him to shut up. 'You've already been twice today,' I said to Gavin.

He shrugged. 'Yeah, I know. I . . . I've just b-been feeling w-w-weird all day . . .'

I gripped his arm hard enough to hurt, and I knew it hurt by the look on his face. 'You better not be late,' I warned him.

'If you are,' Ian chipped in, 'he'll shove those sticks so far up your *b-b-backside* you'll never be able to go again.'

And I turned on him. 'Shut your face, Ian! Just shut up or get lost!'

He looked shocked, and I instantly regretted it, mentally kicking myself. I let go of Gavin, and attempted an apology. 'Look, I'm really sorry. I . . .'

Ian shook his head. 'Forget it,' he said. 'Don't worry about it.'

I took a deep breath. 'It's just . . .' I shrugged. 'You know?'

'Yeah. I do.' He offered me a sympathetic grin. 'I know what this means to you,' he said. 'We all do. But you're kind of taking the fun out of it. We're supposed to be having a good time here.'

I nodded, wincing at the bloated pain in my guts, ignoring the frown on Danny's face. Ian was right. I went to tell Gavin to get going and hurry up, but he'd already scuttled away. I moved over to the nurse's desk and sat down to twiddle my thumbs until he came back.

I wondered if they really did know how much this meant to me, if they knew how important it was for me to be a star. I wondered if Beth had said anything. But now we were only a few minutes away from going up on that stage I felt somehow tied, because there was nothing else I could do; it wasn't as if we could rehearse any more or write new songs.

I hadn't been happy with the sound check, and I didn't like the fact that we had to use the school's PA system, but we hadn't got enough money to hire our own. We'd taken ages getting set up. We'd brought a banner which Danny and I had made the other night to hang behind us on the stage. The original idea had been to have HAPPY written in massive letters, but I'd changed my mind and we'd painted the sunflower instead. It looked great. It was taller than me, standing in a purple pot just like the real one, but with a huge smiley face. The problem was that it had taken us so long to hang it that we'd had very little time for the sound check and I wasn't even sure if I'd be able to hear myself playing because I certainly didn't trust the dodgy old monitor amps we'd been given.

But I told myself to calm down and chill out. I forced myself to believe that nothing could go wrong. The small room was already tight with our nerves and all I was doing was adding to the problem. None of us was in a particularly good mood – we were meant to be friends for God's sake, and I seemed to be making the atmosphere feel somehow dangerous. I began to see why some musicians go in for meditation, or vodka. We needed to release the pressure between us. We needed . . .

And suddenly, as if on cue, the pain in my belly shifted. The lead fart dropped. And when it hit the floor, boy, did it boom! Which was perfect, because there is nothing more certain to get a group of lads laughing, no matter how old they are.

'I'll name that tune in one,' Ian said with tears in his eyes.

We were still giggling when Gavin returned from the toilet. The poor kid didn't know what was going on. He hovered in the doorway looking confused. And flushed. No, not flushed. He was . . .

I pointed at him and was roaring with laughter again. Danny and Ian soon joined in when they realised what I was trying to say. Our drummer had already taken his T-shirt off to expose his ample pre-tanned chest, and had been spending the last couple of minutes in the toilets smearing fresh fake-tanning lotion on his neck, face and arms. It was shiny and still wet in the medical room's dim light, like thick, brown sweat.

'We ready then?' he asked, desperately trying to ignore us, tossing his T-shirt onto the windowsill but missing, pretending nothing was different or wrong, or in the slightest bit amusing.

Danny held his breath to try and curb his laughter. He tried a couple of times before he managed to ask, 'What's all that in aid of?'

'The women,' Gavin said, as if that was the only possible explanation there might be. He might have been blushing, but you couldn't tell. He looked at each of us impatiently. 'Cuh-come on. Shouldn't we be g-getting ready?'

I managed to get a hold of my own laughter, but had to wave my hands to quieten everyone else down. 'Hey,' I shouted. 'Okay. Gav's right, time we got moving, yeah? Now, we've all got everything we need, haven't we? All got set lists, extra strings, plectrums, drumsticks?' They all said they had. 'Good. Okay.' I nodded. 'Let's do it!'

Gavin was carrying the real sunflower to put in his bass drum, and we each in turn touched the purple pot for good luck. Then I led them out of the medical room and across the corridor to the little side door which opened onto the steps at the side of the stage. The door creaked slightly as I opened it and Ian started giggling again like a little boy. I turned to quieten him and saw that Gavin had inadvertently smeared the shoulders of Danny's new shirt with fake tan. I had to bite my hand to keep from laughing out loud myself.

The short narrow stairs were in darkness, loud music enveloped us, but I could still hear the chuffing, snorting noises Ian made through his nose as he tried to hold his laughter in. We jostled against each other, wanting to see, shushing each other noisily. Then the record was swopped for 'Happy Hour' by the Housemartins and all four of us instantly shut up. That song was our cue.

I could just see out into the audience through a gap where the curtains didn't quite meet the side of the stage. I could see dozens of heads bobbing up and down, weaving around in the flashing greens and reds and blues of the disco's lights. There seemed to be so many people out there. I found myself trying to rub my sweaty palms dry on my jeans.

'This is it,' I whispered. 'Now or never. Don't let me down, guys.' And the music began to fade.

Without it I could hear all those people out there. I could

make out a couple of faces, but couldn't see anybody I recognised. I was looking for my father. The teacher working the disco had a microphone; he was reading out the introduction I had written for him. I wanted to tell him I wasn't ready yet. I was frightened I might trip up as I walked on stage, or I might not see the edge and fall off. A string might snap. A fuse might blow. I might forget the song for Christ's sake!

But the teacher didn't care. His bald head glowed orange under the lights.

'Ladies and gentlemen, the moment you have all been waiting for . . .'

I felt my friends go tense around me. Gavin was chewing on his bottom lip, Ian's grip could have choked his bass, and Danny was hissing, 'Oh God, oh God, oh God!'

'The musical debut of the year. The definitive answer to the blues, the only known cure for Saturday night fever – please welcome on stage Cleeston's very own Ian Holmes, Gavin Fisher, Danny Graham and Will Brown.'

Then I was walking across the stage, cheers and applause ringing in my ears, trying to ignore the faces in the crowd. I was picking up my guitar. I had the strap around my shoulders before I really knew what was happening. I was switching on my amp, turning up the volume. I had a plectrum between the first finger and thumb of one hand, the opening chord to 'Chasing Summer' already fretted with the other. Somewhere at the back Gavin was sitting himself down behind his kit. Ian was ready on my left, Danny was waiting on my right. I found myself thinking: this is it. This. Is. It!

I leaned into my microphone.

'Good evening, ladies and gentlemen,' I said. 'We are Happy. And we hope you are too!'

*

Gavin counted us in. The spotlights rotated towards us, flooding the stage in a brilliant white. Danny and I hit the first chord hard. And the alarm went off . . .

Believe it or not, my mind immediately jumped to the conclusion that Danny must be out of tune, but all the stage lights suddenly went out, pitching us into darkness for only a second, then the hall lights came on. The audience were as confused as us at first. A ripple of boos and whistles went through the crowd. Danny, Ian and I stood there looking bewildered and stupid, still playing, but the speakers were silent . . .

Then Gavin shouted, 'There's a fire!' and we saw the smoke at the back of the hall.

The teacher was shouting over his microphone for everyone to leave in an orderly fashion, there was no need to panic, use any available exit. But the floor below us was a scrum. I stood watching what was happening in disbelief. I couldn't get my head round it. I was halfway through the first verse without a single drop of sound emerging from my amp.

But people began jumping up onto the stage, barging past me, heading for the wings and the exit. They were pushing me aside to get by. I was shaking my head at them, shouting that we hadn't finished yet.

Danny grabbed my arm. 'Will, come on. We've got to get going.'

I didn't understand. Gavin was trying to dismantle his kit and we hadn't even finished the first song. Ian told him to leave it and dragged him off into the wings. I could hear the alarm, and there were dozens of kids swarming past me, and I could see the smoke and hear the commotion, but I didn't want to leave the stage. I'd only just got there.

Then some kid tripped over my microphone wire, yanking

it out of the stand. It hit me in the mouth with an audible crunch.

'Bring your guitar,' Danny was yelling. 'Keep hold of it.'

Ian's amp had been kicked over, Gavin's drums pushed and shoved and had toppled in a heap. Our sunflower banner had been ripped down. It had taken us three hours to make.

There was a lot of noise and shouting. I let the crush of bodies carry me along down the narrow steps and out into the corridor. The alarm was so loud, so *off key*. I was jabbed and elbowed and kicked as everyone fought for the exit. I tried holding my guitar above my head so it wouldn't get damaged. Everybody was pushing and shoving. I was forced up against the wall. It was difficult to walk without standing on somebody else's feet, I was worried I might fall and not be able to get back up, but the flow of people took me quickly along the corridor. Danny was by my side. I couldn't read the look on his face.

We burst out of the red double doors onto the school field. The night air was cold against my face, and I realised my mouth was bleeding from where my microphone had struck me. A whole crowd was milling around in the darkness. An adult, maybe a teacher, was trying to organise people. 'Stay with your friends. Make sure everybody's here. Group together.'

We pushed our way through. Ian and Gavin were standing near the back with a bass guitar and a snare drum between them. Gav also had the sunflower in its purple pot. How on earth he'd rescued it I'll never know, but for once it didn't make me smile. They were looking back at the school building, looking above it at the night sky. I turned to look too, and saw the pall of black smoke as it slowly curled above the hall's roof. It rose higher, grew larger as I watched, fattening, thickening, and it blotted out the stars one by one.

I felt completely and utterly useless. I watched the smoke filling up the already dark night and felt so very tired. My guitar was heavy around my shoulders so I took it off and put it on the cold ground. My face hurt, so I held my hand against it to try and ease the pain. When I took it away my fingers were sticky with blood. My friends looked awkward. They didn't know how to react to me, what to say to help, what to do for the best. They all looked embarrassed by me being there, so I walked away. I didn't know what to say to them either. If they were feeling as messed-up as I was, then there was nothing I could say. I felt as if I was falling, as if I'd been pushed off a great height and was still waiting to hit the ground.

I walked away from the bustling crowd. There was an excited nervousness on people's faces because they'd escaped. They were safe now and could just simply log all the juicy details to swap in stories with each other later on. 'Remember the fire? I was there that night.' Everybody would remember the fire.

I walked around the side of the school building. I walked past some tennis courts and sat down on a little brick wall beside the path. The shadow of the school fell over me. I could hear the fire engines now. I remembered I'd left my guitar, but at least it wasn't in the hall. I guessed it was the last we'd see of my microphone and the amplifiers. I kind of felt sorry for Gavin. What if they couldn't get to his kit in time? This would be the second bass drum he'd lost in only a few months.

The disappointment was a dull ache. It swelled up inside me, like a balloon two sizes too big for my body to hold in. I had no idea which would pop first; me or it. Everybody would remember the fire, but who would remember me?

The stale, metallic taste of my blood was unpleasant, my

throbbing mouth sharp and painful. I wondered if I needed stitches. And would I have a scar? Would I for ever be marked by my own microphone? Would it leave its imprint on my face for everybody to see for the rest of my life?

I thought:

'Scarred by ambition, is that what this means?
Branded by failure, marked by the dream.'

I thought it might sound good in a song one day. And it struck me as strange that even now I couldn't switch off that part of my head.

There was a lot of noise coming from around the other side of the school. It sounded as though the fire brigade had arrived; someone was barking orders, the fire engine rumbled and growled. But I didn't want to go back to see what was happening. I stayed sitting on the wall beside the tennis courts in the dark. I didn't think I could face anyone just yet. I didn't want anybody telling me how sorry they were this had happened. I didn't even want to know how the fire had started. I didn't care. What the hell did it matter anyway? I'd still failed, right?

A few minutes passed in the cold. My mouth had stopped bleeding and I licked my lips tentatively. I could still hear people's voices above the sound of the fire engine. Then I saw Danny coming towards me. He was carrying my guitar. His new shirt flapped open because the buttons had been ripped off. He stood next to me and shivered, unsure whether or not to sit down.

'Your dad's looking for you,' he said.

I didn't reply. I ignored him. I looked at my huge hands in my lap.

'He's worried about you.'

I shrugged. Maybe I'd go see him if nobody else was going to be there. But I knew they all would be. There'd be a big crowd of them. Beth and my grandparents, Danny's mum and dad, his sister, Gav, Ian, Mr Fisher. Hell, maybe even Fitch and Mr Holloway too! But why should I have to talk to them? I simply wasn't interested in sympathy or explanations or promises that everything would be all right the next time.

Danny held out my guitar. 'Do you want this?'

I nodded and took it from him. 'Thanks.' As I did I saw the look on his face and realised that he was just as upset as I was.

He had been as excited by this gig as I had. I wasn't the only one who'd worked hard at trying to get this band off the ground. So maybe I'd let him down. But I still felt as though it was me who had risked the most. Risked it, and lost it.

'Are you going to come over?'

I shook my head.

'Do you want me to tell your dad where you are?'

I shook my head again. 'I'll see him later,' I said. 'I'm just a bit . . .' I shrugged. 'You know?' I looked up at him. His eyes were wet. He was going to start crying in a minute. And I knew I couldn't face it if he did.

I jumped quickly to my feet. 'Leave me alone,' I told him. 'I'm going for a walk. Go away.' But it was no good because I'd already started crying myself.

Part Two

Danny

THE SPLIT

Will's act is a tough one to follow, though like it or not, that's exactly what everybody expected me to do.

It was New Year's Eve. It was also my sister and Ian's engagement party and I reckoned I was the only person in the universe who was drinking Coke. I hung around in the kitchen feeling sorry for myself. Everyone else was in the living room: aunties and uncles, cousins, workmates and neighbours, from both Ian and Deborah's side. I couldn't believe my mum had allowed so many people into the house, although she did seem honestly pleased at the prospect of having Ian as a son-in-law, and everybody had obediently taken their shoes off when they came in. I'd spent most of the night making name tags for them. Even Gav was here, drinking Babycham from a pint glass last time I'd seen him. He was eighteen now, his birthday actually falling on Christmas Day, so I was the only one not old enough to drink. And maybe my mum had long ago forgiven Ian for the beer stain on her carpet, but it certainly looked as though I'd be out in the cold for several months yet. The only person who'd been invited who hadn't turned up was Will. At least if he had bothered to appear we could have shared Cokes, because he wasn't eighteen until a whole month after me.

I was quite surprised when Ian proposed to Deborah; I'd assumed things between them had been going pear-shaped because of his strange moodiness for the few weeks before he'd asked her. I was pleased for him now, even though I wouldn't have wished a lifetime shackled to my sister on anybody; it meant I'd still be in touch with him even if Happy was going to fall apart.

I finished my drink and went to the fridge to get another. There was a stack of beer in there and only one Coke. Surely, I thought, surely I should take a beer in case somebody else wants that last can of Coke later on. It wouldn't be right to take the last one, now would it? I decided not.

Listening all the time to the chatter and laughter coming from the living room I cracked open the beer can and took a swig. It wasn't the point that I didn't like beer as much as Coke. I tried to drink it all down as quickly as possible. I wasn't even half finished when I heard someone coming. I nearly choked. My mum was going to kill me. I jumped across the kitchen in panic and threw the can into the sink.

It was only Gav. I scowled at him and tried to rescue what was left of the beer. Just my luck – it had dribbled away down the plug hole. I swore under my breath and went back to the fridge. I snatched at the Coke nastily, rocking the shelf, as if it was the fridge's fault all along for tempting me.

'Why're you drinking that?' Gav asked. His cheeks were flushed with booze, his stutter miraculously cured.

'Because I like it,' I told him. I looked at the strange, murky, almost milky liquid he had in the glass tankard his dad had bought him for his birthday/Christmas. 'What've you got?'

'Baileys,' he said. He took another gulp. 'Ian's having a good time. And your sister's not as bad as I thought she'd be. She's all right looking. Nice eyes.'

Now I knew he was drunk. 'If you say so, Gav.'

'What was it Will used to call her? The Taxi?'

'The Tractor.'

'That's it. I remember. Big backside, but small . . .'

I nodded quickly. 'Yeah. Yeah, that's right, Gav.'

He laughed loudly, nearly spilling his drink, almost falling over but using the cooker to keep himself upright. 'But she's not bad. Ian's done all right for himself.'

'You being the expert on women of course.'

He nodded. 'Of course.' He took a mouthful of Baileys. 'She's not bad at all.' He looked me up and down with blood-shot eyes. 'Did you get the brains of the family then?' Which was a pretty good joke for Gav, considering. He thought it was the funniest thing he had ever heard. He laughed so hard that he threw up into the kitchen sink.

He groaned. He slid down the pine-effect MFI unit to the floor, his cheeks turning green right before my eyes. I needed to get him to the bathroom. Quick. Before my mum saw him. But there was no way I could carry him there by myself. What was I going to do?

'Please, Gav. Don't puke again. Not till I can get you to the bathroom, okay? Gav, are you listening to me?'

He nodded the tiniest amount.

I grabbed a casserole dish out of the nearest cupboard and shoved it onto the floor beside him anyway, then went through to the living room to find Ian.

He was standing with Deborah, holding her hand, sur-rounded by the guests. He was wearing his best suit and tie, beaming big smiles at all the attention he was getting. My mum's voice was the loudest in the room, telling everybody about the promotion he'd just been given at the bank. I'd not seen her so jolly in ages. I didn't dare spoil her night with news of Gav.

I tried to make my way over to Ian and Deborah but rela-tives kept stopping me and asking daft questions about what it felt like having my elder sister getting engaged. 'Your turn next,' they told me. I smiled politely and kept moving until I could tug on Ian's sleeve.

'Hey, Danny. Come and join me in a toast,' he beamed. 'My health.'

'Not now, Ian. I need your help.'

'No worries,' he told me grabbing me by the shoulders. 'Seeing as we're almost family now. What can I do for you, little brother?'

'Gav's chundered in the kitchen. You can shut up and help me carry him to the bathroom before my mum sees him.'

Ian's smile slipped.

'Quick.'

He nodded, whispered something in Deborah's ear, then followed me as I headed for the door.

Gav had managed to fill the casserole dish by the time we made it to the kitchen. Ian swore and rolled his eyes.

'What's he been drinking?' he asked.

'Babycham and Baileys,' I said. 'Pints of.'

'Oh, for God's sake . . .' He knelt down. 'Gav. Gavin, can you hear me?' The drummer groaned. 'Okay,' Ian said. 'I'll carry him over my shoulder, you follow me with the bowl.'

I emptied the casserole dish into the sink and rinsed everything away. I had to force the larger chunks down the plughole with my fingers. What a way to celebrate New Year! Ian used the fireman's lift to get Gav over his shoulder and I then followed with the dish only an inch or so below his face as Ian, huffing and puffing all the way, carried him up the stairs. Luckily we made it to the bathroom without any mishaps. Ian put Gavin down so that his head hung over the bath, filled the dish with cold water, and tipped it over the lad's head. Gav coughed and spluttered. But Ian kept him held down for another dishful before letting him sag to the floor.

'Wuh-what did you do that for?'

'Because you're drunk,' Ian told him.

'Are you all right now?' I asked. 'You puked in the kitche.

Gav shook his head. 'I . . . I f-feel like sh-sh-sh . . .'

'You look like it too,' Ian said. He sat down on the floor next to him. 'What's up, Gav? You've never struck me as the hard-drinking type before.'

The drummer shrugged. He looked miserable.

'Come on, what is it? Some woman stood you up or something?'

He shook his head.

Ian and I waited for Gav to speak. It was obvious something was wrong.

He rubbed his wet and spiky red hair. 'It's Happy,' he said.

Ian and I looked at each other.

Gav looked at his hands. 'We haven't had a rehearsal in ages,' he said. 'I've t-tried ruh-ringing Will, but his grandma says he's not in all the t-t-time. And yuh-you two h-h-haven't been in touch all Christmas, and . . . and I j-just don't know what's h-happening any more.' He looked at us both. 'Are . . . Are w-we still in a band, or what?'

We both shrugged.

'It's all right for y-you,' he told us. 'Ian's got a j-j-job, and Duh-Danny's good at school. But . . . But wuh-what have I got? I've only got the band.'

And that was when both Gav and Ian turned to me for the answers, just like they'd always turned to Will. It wasn't fair. I tried to protest. I'd never made the decisions. And I didn't see why I had to now.

I hadn't actually spoken to Will since the night of the gig. Over the following few days before we'd broken up for Christmas he'd only turned up at the comp if he'd had a lesson to go to, and then had disappeared back home as soon as it was over. Which had been fine by me. I guess we'd both been doing our best to avoid each other.

'Maybe you should give him a ring?' Ian said. Gav agreed.

I pulled a face. I wasn't so sure.

'Have you seen him over the holidays at all?' Ian asked, and I shook my head. 'Why not?'

I knew exactly why not. I still shrugged, however, not willing to share, not wanting them to know the real reason why he'd walked away and left me when I'd taken his guitar back to him.

'You know, for best mates, you two certainly seem to hate each other's guts sometimes.' Ian shook his head at me. 'You've known each other for ages. You're probably the only one he'd talk to anyway.'

I sat on the floor with them, leaning back against the toilet. 'Maybe not. He's changed. You know how serious he got, as if the band was the only thing in the world that mattered.'

Ian nodded. 'Yeah, and you know why, don't you?'

'Of course I do,' I said. 'It's because he reckons he's different to everybody else. He wants to be famous.' I shocked myself with how bitter I sounded.

'Yeah,' Ian said. 'But that's only because of his—'

He was cut short by my surprised howl of pain as the bathroom door swung sharply open and whacked into my legs. My sister poked her head inside.

'That's a stupid place to sit,' she told me.

I clutched my leg, hissing in agony. 'You did that on purpose.'

'How was I to know the three of you would be sprawled on the bathroom floor?' she asked. She tutted at the look on my face. 'I'm sure it's not that bad, Daniel.'

'It kills.'

'Well! it's lucky your big sister's a nurse then, isn't it?' She gave me a sarcastic smile, but didn't offer to do any of the said nursing for me. She looked across at Ian. 'People are asking where you are.'

'Tell them I'm in the toilet. Tell them I'm practising how to look after little children.'

Deborah wasn't amused.

'I'll be down in a minute,' he assured her.

'I hope it's not more *band-talk*,' she said. 'Surely that's dead and buried by now.'

'Gav's not very well,' Ian told her.

'He looks all right to me,' she said.

Then, to prove just how rough he was, Gav chose that exact moment to be sick on Ian's new suit jacket.

'Oh, Gav, no! Not my suit!'

Deborah pulled a face of disgust. She turned to me. '*Don't* let Mum see him like that,' she threatened, as if everything was my fault. 'Spoil her night and I'll never forgive you.'

She slammed the door and was gone before I had time to defend myself. I rubbed at the pain in my leg and dreamed of how pleasant times were going to be when she left home.

Ian was trying to rinse his jacket off under the bath tap. He was the one stuttering now. 'You . . . you complete . . . and utter . . .'

'Sorry,' Gav murmured.

Ian eventually managed to clean himself up as well as possible, although he decided not to put his jacket back on. He asked me to hang it in the airing cupboard to dry for him. I did it quickly and came back to the bathroom to find him helping Gav to his feet.

'You'd better ring his dad,' Ian told me.

'Wuh-what about Huh-Happy?' Gav insisted.

I bit my lip. 'I guess I'll have to talk to Will if you really want me to.'

'You may have to do without me, I'm afraid, guys,' Ian said.

'Why? What's wrong?'

'You know, with this promotion at work and everything, I just don't think I'm going to have as much time.'

'Don't you want to p-p-play any more?' Gav asked him.

Ian didn't answer.

'Don't you want to be a rock 'n' roll star?' I asked, trying to make him smile, but still sounding bitter.

'I don't really want to be a dad . . .' he said quietly.

I felt a chill run down my spine. 'You what?'

He shrugged, shuffled his feet. 'Debs is pregnant.'

'Oh, God . . .' I felt like I'd been punched in the stomach. I had to grab the towel rail for support. I couldn't quite get my head round it. I tried to picture her standing in the bathroom doorway only a couple of minutes ago. 'She doesn't look pregnant.'

'Not yet.'

'What about my mum? Does she . . . ?'

He shook his head.

'Oh, God . . .'

'We found out about a month ago.'

I now suddenly realised why Ian had been kind of weird at the run-up to the gig. 'God, Ian. What . . . ? I mean . . . You know?'

He sighed. 'Yeah, I know. We just haven't found the right time to tell anyone yet. Please don't say anything.'

'God, no! No way.'

He put Gav's arm over his shoulder to keep the drummer upright. 'So I'm sorry, Gav. But Happy's the least of my worries right now.'

Gav nodded, but seemed too drunk to properly understand. 'She's not b-bad,' he said. 'You've done well for yourself.'

'What do you want to do about it, then?' I asked.

'I love playing with you lot,' Ian said. 'Hey! I want to be famous too, you know. It'll sure beat sitting behind that desk in the Royal Bank of Scotland all day. But I'm going to have to put Debs first. And the baby. I can't practise every night of the week again like last time. It was a bit of fun, Danny, a real good laugh. Until Will went over the top on us.'

I helped him get Gav to the door and out onto the landing.

'I guess I've got to grow up sometime,' he said. 'Happy isn't going to pay my wages, is it? Not when we're playing gigs at school discos. And it certainly isn't going to help me raise a kid.'

I nodded slowly. I couldn't hide my disappointment.

'You know, if Will does decide to get us back together, we'll never find another bassist as good as you.'

'I'd be offended if you did,' he laughed.

'You can't leave the band,' Gav whined. 'We n-need you.'

'And how would you know?' Ian asked. 'You're drunk.'

But Gav had a point. It had always been about the four of us, hadn't it?

Alone with Beth

Maybe, given time, I would have phoned Will. Maybe not. Who knows? Maybe things would have turned out differently if I had. Maybe not. But it was Beth who stopped me from doing it.

I was coming to the end of a long, long day of deliveries. It's funny, isn't it, how parents complain about you not revising for your exams because of, say, playing your guitar in a rock band? But they think it's perfectly all right for you to miss that self-same revision if you're doing *them* a favour. I could have argued that my mocks started in a couple of days and got out of doing it, I suppose, but I had a plan. You see, I knew that sooner or later my mum had to find out about what Deborah and Ian had been up to with the lights off, and I simply wanted to make sure I was in her good books when she did. I was determined not to catch any of the fall-out when she went BOOM!

So I'd spent a cold and wet Saturday afternoon taking out the deliveries. Now I was ready for a shower and a night slouched in front of the telly. It was half-six already and I'd only just finished. It was raining and dark as I drove along the High Street heading back to the shop.

I had to stop at a pelican crossing. I was yawning and in a world of my own when somebody thumped on the van's side window. I jumped in my seat. And Beth peered in, laughing at me. I blushed, feeling like a sap, and reached across to open the door for her.

'Sorry, Danny. Didn't mean to make you jump.' She smiled at me. 'I don't suppose you're going my way, are you?'

'Yeah. Of course,' I lied, not knowing which way she was going at all.

'You're a life-saver,' she told me, climbing in.

As I pulled away from the crossing she tried to arrange her long coat around her so that she didn't make herself any wetter.

'Haven't seen you for a while,' she said. 'How're you doing? Good Christmas and that?'

'All right, yeah.' I watched her out of the corner of my eye as I drove. 'You?'

'Don't ask.'

I shrugged and didn't. She pulled the sun visor down and used the little mirror as she tried to push her wet hair back into some sort of order. She leaned in close to it and inspected her smudged make-up, tutting under her breath. She had dribbles of rainwater running down her cheeks and off her forehead, dripping into her eyes. Her mascara ran with it.

She sighed. 'I think I hate him,' she said.

I turned to look at her. 'Who?'

'Who'd you think?'

She snapped the sun visor up again and leaned back in her seat. She closed her eyes. The silence between us spun out uncomfortably. I kept glancing at her from out of the corner of my eye. She brushed some water from her cheek wearily. I thought she was the most beautiful girl on the planet. I always had.

I cleared my throat. 'Er, do you want taking home?' I asked.

She shook her head. 'Where're you going, Danny? Anywhere interesting?'

'Just to the shop. I've got to take a couple of bouquets back that I wasn't able to deliver.'

'Yeah?' She turned to look in the back. 'Any of them up for grabs, are they?'

'Sorry, no. They'll have to go out again on Monday.'

'Pity,' she said. 'I could have done with something to cheer me up.' She leaned back in her seat again. 'Well, Danny. I'm sorry to say you're stuck with me for the evening. I told my mum I wasn't going to be home till later, and I don't want her calling me a liar now, do I?' She raised her eyebrows at me, waiting to see if I was going to argue.

I managed to force a shrug, playing it cool. Inside I was happier than I'd been in a long time.

I parked outside the front of the shop and ran to unlock the front door, ducking my head against the pouring rain. I was hurrying and briefly considered carrying more than one bouquet at a time from the back of the van to the shop. Unfortunately my mother's commands were so deeply ingrained I still scuttled in and out with the five bouquets one at a time. I'd been shouted at too often for carrying two together, holding them upside down by their stems. My mum said you carried them like they were babies, and you didn't carry a baby dangling by its legs now, did you? I was hurrying though because I didn't want Beth to be waiting too long for me. I didn't want her to change her mind.

It took me about ten minutes to sort the bouquets out and dump them in water to wait until Monday. I was about to switch the lights off and leave when Beth appeared behind me.

'Chicken chow mein,' she smiled, holding up a steaming plastic carrier bag with the words 'Lucky Star Takeaway' written on the side. 'Mr Li was even kind enough to give us some plastic forks,' she said.

'It'll be cold by the time we get home,' I told her.

She rolled her eyes and tutted at me. 'You lock the van and I'll set the table, okay?'

'Oh, right,' I said, looking dumb.

'Go on then. Move yourself.'

I did as I was told, and when I got back inside I closed the door which connected the front of the shop with the back room so that nobody could see in from the road. Beth had cleared the wooden table and grabbed a stool and an upturned crate for us to sit on. She took her coat off and hung it up to drip-dry while I got the little electric heater going and aimed it at us as best I could. I thought it only polite to take the crate and sat myself down.

She passed me a can of Diet Coke, opened a can of her own, held it up and said, 'Cheers.'

I grinned. 'Yeah. Cheers.' We touched cans. The foil container full of chicken chow mein sat between us in the middle of the table and we tucked in.

I ate quickly, and not only because all I'd had to eat since lunch was a king-size Snickers. Mr Li was a genius; it tasted wonderful.

'It's been years since I've had Chinese,' I said, my mouth full of gorgeous noodles, clearly enjoying myself.

'Is it? I thought you would've virtually lived on the stuff with it only being next door.'

'My mum's not a fan,' I explained.

Beth nodded. 'Figures.' She spotted a massive slab of chicken and got to it before me. 'Seems such a waste though,' she said popping it in her mouth.

'Tell me about it.'

She was drying out now. She was wearing a blue V-necked jumper, dark jeans. The wet and cold had left a rosy glow in her cheeks. She had a plastic hairslide holding back her almost non-existent fringe. It was bright yellow, shaped into the word 'Tuesday' and I wondered if she had one for every day of the week – until I remembered it was Saturday. I tried not to stare at her, but it was a fight. I thought about Will. I'd never admitted how jealous I was of him for seeing Beth. She looked stunning surrounded by all the bright and colourful flowers. She was so beautiful it scared me half to death.

I dropped a mushroom on the way to my mouth. It hit the table and rolled to the edge, leaving a wet trail, then plopped to the floor. I was left with an empty fork and my big, expectant mouth hanging open. For some reason Beth found this particularly funny. She almost choked on the chunky piece of chicken she'd pinched as she was overcome with giggles. Which only made her laugh even more, until she had tears in her eyes, making them sparkle. I kicked the mushroom under the table as nonchalantly as possible and laughed along too. Will was a fool, I decided, quite possibly the stupidest person I knew – because he'd let her go.

We talked about school, and the start of the mocks next week. We talked about our Christmas presents. We talked about university and about her dog, Walter. We had a brief fight for the last piece of chicken; she won by purposely snapping my fork. Then all too quickly the meal was over. We sat back feeling stuffed and content. But I knew it wouldn't last; I knew she really wanted to talk about Will.

'Have you seen much of him recently?' she asked.

'Not since the gig,' I admitted.

'How come?'

'We've just not been in touch. Both been a bit busy, I suppose. You've seen him today though, haven't you?'

She nodded. 'I was on my way back from his house when I saw you. I wanted to talk to him; I just wanted to see if he was okay. But he wasn't interested. I guess I was really hoping we could maybe patch things up, but he couldn't get rid of me quick enough just so he could start playing his guitar again.'

That kind of surprised me. I don't know why. 'He's still playing his guitar?'

She took a sip of her Diet Coke. 'Yeah. Still playing guitar, still writing songs, still dreaming of being a star.'

'Is he thinking about getting the band back together?'

'No idea. Why? Do you want him to?'

I shrugged, which was a much more honest answer than it looked. 'I kind of miss it,' I said.

'So you'd do it if he asked?'

'I don't know. Maybe. I'd like to prove everybody wrong who's been taking the mick ever since the gig. I mean, it wasn't our fault, was it?'

She shook her head. 'Will seems to think it was that Richard Fitch kid.'

'Seriously?'

'That's what he said to me. Fitch did it out of revenge and jealousy according to Will.'

'Even Fitch isn't that much of a nutter, is he?'

'Will seems to think so.' She drank from her can again. 'And it seems only fair after all. You stole his drummer, stole his gig, and wrecked his car. If you look at it like that then it's almost justice that he tried to spoil your gig and kill you at the same time.'

I was shocked and it must have showed on my face.

Beth tutted at me and shook her head. 'Joke, Danny. Joke.'

Admittedly the fire was somebody's fault. The fire brigade, or the police, or Inspector Morse or whoever, had said that it had been caused by some moron dropping their fag end too close to the hall's curtains. But did I believe it could have been done on purpose? By Fitch? I wasn't sure. Although, whoever it had been, they hadn't just destroyed Stonner Secondary's hall, but most of our gear as well. I guess it was sheer fluke that nobody got hurt.

It had all been made worse for us, and all the more humiliating, the following day when the Cleeston *Evening Telegraph* had made a most remarkable mistake. They had two articles about what had happened, and somehow managed to mix them up. One was the serious, analytical front page story dealing with the terrible event and talking about how the school would cope for the sake of the pupils. The second was destined for 'Big Tony's Music Review', supposedly talking about Happy as Cleeston's newest rock band, but for obvious reasons having very little to say about our music, and instead ending up as a light-hearted look at our public failure under the headline THE HOTTEST NEW BAND IN TOWN. Somewhere along the line, however, the articles were accidentally swapped, and we'd made front-page news.

'How are Ian and Gavin?' Beth asked. 'I haven't seen either of them over Christmas. I don't suppose they've talked to Will, have they?'

'Gav's tried,' I said. 'I think Ian's got a few too many of his own problems, though.'

She looked interested, but was polite enough not to ask.

'The thing is,' I said, 'the thing that really winds me up about Will, is that he seems to think he's the only one who's upset by what happened. I mean, he always had this attitude that he was the only one who really cared about Happy, which wasn't true, and now he's locking himself away and acting like some sort of tormented artist, all lonely and depressed.'

'I think it's because of his dad.'

'What's it got to do with his dad?'

'Well, because he really wanted to impress him, didn't he? Maybe what happened at the gig really hurt him.'

'Yeah, but it really hurt me as well. I was disappointed too.'

And the disappointment had been a killer. It had been like playing Postman's Knock with those blonde twins from the year below us *and* the new student teacher with the low-cut tops only to have your mum catch you before you'd even had chance to pucker up. The nerves and excitement and anticipation before the gig had taken me up incredibly high, but the heavy, heavy disappointment had pulled me down so very low so very quickly. It was like an anticlimax with knives.

'You don't know what it was like on that stage,' I said to her. 'You know, when we first walked on and everybody was clapping and cheering, it felt unbelievable. And the thing was that we knew we were good. We'd written some fantastic songs, but we didn't even get a chance to play them.'

I didn't tell her what it had felt like when the fire alarm had gone off and everybody started climbing onto the stage to get away. I didn't tell her it had been the scariest moment in my life, with everybody pushing and shoving, fighting to get out of the hall. It was like the world was falling apart around me. And I didn't know what to do to stop it; I'd just known we all had to get out of there. My head had been way too small to handle all the crazy emotions at once. What was I? Excited? Or nervous? Confused, but scared to death and disappointed? At the time I had no idea what on earth I should be feeling.

I guess that was why I'd cried afterwards. It had been the only thing I could do to handle what was churning around inside my head. It had been the only thing I could do to let it all escape.

And Will had seen me cry. But he'd walked away.

Beth shrugged. 'To tell you the truth, Danny, the whole Happy business is getting on my nerves.' She saw the shocked look on my face, but carried on regardless. 'I'm fed up of hearing about it. It's caused nothing but hassle if you ask me. Will's been treating me like dirt ever since he got that stupid guitar and decided he wanted to be a rock star.'

'I never thought you two would split up,' I said.

She shook her head. '*I* never wanted to. But I should have known better.' She paused, drinking from her can. Then she asked, 'How come you never asked me out, Danny?'

What the . . . ? I didn't know what to say. I blushed. But Beth simply sat on her stool looking at me as if all she'd asked me about was the weather or something.

'Because you were going out with Will,' I said quietly.

She was staring at me. 'Before that. You've known me as long as he has. How come you never invited me to the pictures?'

I fidgeted uncomfortably and the crate I was sitting on creaked with my weight.

'Didn't you want to?'

I was looking at my hands. 'Yeah. Of course.'

'So why didn't you?'

I stood up quickly, alarmed at the sudden, unexpected swing in the conversation. I crumpled the foil container, spilling the last few dregs of chow mein gravy, and walked over to the bin with it, dropping it in. I had my back to her. 'Just, you know . . . Just thought you'd say no.'

'I would have done,' she agreed. 'Back then, anyway. No reason for you not to have asked me though. I used to put on my best make-up whenever I knew I was going to see you.'

'Really?'

But she just gave me one of her looks, and I wanted to die. I was beginning to think I'd never felt so uncomfortable in my whole life.

'Anyway, listen,' I said. 'I really ought to get the van home. I mean, in case my dad needs it or something.'

'Why do I always end up with lads like Will?' Beth asked no one in particular, staring at the flowers all around her. She got up and walked over to a tub full of large daisies, and picked the biggest she could find. 'I must attract them, wouldn't you agree?' She sat back down and plucked the white petals one by one, dropping them to the floor. 'I must be a magnet for them.'

I strode over to the table with a cloth and tried mopping up the gravy I'd spilled. I was thinking this was all going wrong somehow. I was thinking, Rewind, rewind!

'I should have been home ages ago,' I said. 'You know what my mum's like, she'll . . .'

'I'm sure it'd be good to see some nice, decent, boring bloke for once.' She looked up from her daisy. 'What d'you reckon, Danny? Do you think you're boring enough for me?'

'Beth, look . . .' I started. But stopped there.

She was crying.

I moved to her, but didn't touch her. I didn't know what to do.

'Danny . . . Oh, God, I'm sorry. I'm so sorry.' She dropped the daisy and wept into her hands.

'No, please . . . Don't worry about it.' I kind of hovered there feeling awkward, useless . . . stupid.

'That was spiteful of me. I'm so sorry. I didn't mean to hurt you. I just . . .' She tried in vain to wipe her tears away. 'God! I'm such a cow!'

I fumbled in my pocket for a tissue, but didn't have one. I knelt on the cold concrete floor beside her and touched her shoulder.

She looked at me with her huge, green eyes, tears glistening in them. She sniffed loudly, a big, fat snorter, and half-giggled at it, half-cried. She apologised again. She put her arms around my neck and rested her head on my shoulder. 'I like you, Danny. Why couldn't you have asked me out first?'

I looked at her, touched her hair. Did I dare . . . ?

'I'm sorry,' she said again. 'Look at the state of me. I feel awful. What on earth would you want with a girl like me?' She tried to smile, but it was crooked.

And I kissed her. There didn't seem to be anything else I could do. She tasted of chicken chow mein.

THE DRUMMER

I'd been trying to avoid Gavin, but he caught up with me a few days after my mocks had finished. It wasn't that I didn't like him any more, and I honestly felt bad about dodging into classrooms or toilets when I saw him coming towards me down the corridor, but I knew he'd be asking about Happy all the time. Asking if I'd mentioned getting back together to Will just yet. It wasn't something I wanted to talk about.

He was waiting for me when I came out of English one afternoon. I immediately realised I had nowhere to hide, and then felt horrible for even thinking about wanting to. We walked together over to the sixth-form block.

'D'you reckon Will's okay?' he asked.

It wasn't the question I was expecting. 'I don't know,' I said. 'I think so. But I haven't seen him properly in ages,' I added quickly, covering myself. 'He's hardly ever here. I haven't really had chance to talk to him just yet.'

'D'you know if he's still interested in music?'

Again the question surprised me. 'Well, yeah. Probably. But like I said, I haven't . . .'

'I – I don't get it why he hasn't called me,' Gav said. 'I keep calling him, but his grandma says he's out all the time. D'you reckon he's got another band?'

Now this was definitely something I hadn't thought about.

'You've got to talk to him, Danny,' Gav told me. 'Plu-please. You're his best mate, he'll listen to y-you.'

I nodded. But I didn't phone, even though I'd agreed twice now that I would.

I didn't want to talk to Will because I didn't want to tell him about me and Beth. I let the weeks pass and avoided him like I avoided Gavin. But I did wonder exactly what was going on with him at the moment. What was it that kept him clear of the rest of us? Why hadn't he tried to get Happy back together? Was it really because he had another band now? But I couldn't believe that was true.

I decided that Will was still playing at his 'tormented artist' role. He wanted us to think he was locking himself away in a room and creating rock masterpieces which he hoped would bring the world of pop music to its knees. And the more I thought about it, the more I believed it was true. He'd lost interest in everything but his songs.

The problem was, thinking these things made me miss Happy even more. I missed meeting up on Tuesday and Thursday nights and blasting out our tunes. Playing those songs had made me feel so special. I'd felt like a rock star even in the back room of my mum and dad's flower shop or Gavin's dirty garage. But I had Beth now, I told myself, and I was desperate not to make the same mistakes Will had because she made me feel so very special too. I told myself it had never really been a serious dream of mine anyway. Yes, I'd wanted to be a rock star at the time. Yes, I'd thought it would be the most fantastic thing ever, but I'd never truly believed I'd become one. It had only been wishful thinking, hadn't it? Childish dreams, a bit of a lark . . . Hadn't it?

Then again, maybe I didn't know what I wanted.

It was thoughts like this which sent me back to the music shop. I went behind Beth's back, for some reason deciding not to tell her what I was doing. I was supposed to be on my way to her house, and it was loads quicker to get there if I went down Carvard Avenue past the comp, but I was curious to see if the red Gibson had been sold yet, because I had enough money put aside to buy it now. Now that I didn't have a band to play it in. I'd hated having to ask for my deposit back; I'd felt such a fool. And I'd wanted that guitar *so* badly.

It was the second week in March. Not that you could tell – spring still seemed miles away. It had snowed over the weekend and everything was slushy and grey and cold. Fast forward to the summer, that's what I thought! I saw the white Escort parked a little further up the road, and noticed there were some lads sitting inside, but it didn't click who it could be at first. I was wondering what I would do if the guitar was still there. Would I really buy it? Would I go straight round to Will's house and shout, 'Hey, Will! Are you happy, or what?' Of course I wouldn't, I told myself. Of course not. I didn't want to get involved in stuff like that again. But I thought it was a perfectly reasonable question to ask myself all the same.

I was kind of nervous when I pushed open the door and went to step inside. I'd purposely avoided looking through the window in case I saw it (or didn't see it) hanging there, because I didn't know what I'd do if it was (or wasn't). I wanted to wait until I was inside, I wanted to surprise myself. So I didn't see Fitch about to step out into the street. And pushed the door right in his face.

It hit him hard. He staggered two or three steps backwards in surprise, then fell heavily onto his backside. His look of shock would have seemed comical on somebody less dangerous.

'Oh, God! Fitch! God, I'm sorry. Are you okay?'

He swore at me and put his hand up to his nose to check for blood. 'Watch where you're going, you stupid . . .' He suddenly realised who I was, and scrambled to his feet.

My first instinct was to run, but I couldn't get my legs into gear quickly enough. He grabbed me by the front of my coat.

The shop's owner must have seen what had happened and shouted from behind his counter, 'Hey! No fighting near the guitars.' So Fitch hauled the door open and dragged me out into the street. He was swearing and cursing at me, calling me every name under the sun. I was still apologising. 'I didn't see you. I'm sorry, Fitch. I'm really sorry.'

He forced me down onto my knees in the wet slush on the pavement. I tried to stand, not willing to simply lie there and take a beating if there was a way to escape. He shoved me down again, harder, and my shoes slipped on the dirty snow, sending me sprawling. I got a face full. The thought flashed through my mind that I was dead now. This kid was a nutter. He was going to kick me to pieces. I held my hands above my head, trying to protect myself. I kept apologising, telling him I hadn't seen him. I was trying to get to my knees and then my feet without using my hands and I was sliding and skidding all over the place. He was going to tear me apart.

'Don't, Fitch!'

I recognised that voice, but I didn't look up. The blow I was expecting never fell, but I stayed where I was.

'Leave him alone.'

'He shoved a door in my face,' Fitch protested.

'He's not worth it.'

'He could've broken my nose.'

'Cuh-come on. He probably didn't do it on p-purpose.'

I looked up from Fitch's massive DMs to see Gavin climbing out of the white Escort. He walked over to us. 'He's a m-m-mate,' he said.

'Not of me,' Fitch told him. He spat in my hair to prove it. I was just thankful he hadn't hit me yet. 'I owe him for all the grief him and his yeti friend gave me last year.'

My knees were beginning to freeze. I slowly stood up, careful not to slip again, and wary of Fitch's raised fist.

'You all r-right, Danny?' Gav asked.

I nodded, wiping the cold slush off me as best I could.

'How's your ugly mate and your pathetic rock band?' Fitch asked me, prodding me in the chest. 'What's it like having someone steal your drummer off you?'

I looked at Gav, confused. He was looking at his feet. The other two members of Fitch's band also climbed out of the Escort, but they didn't come over.

'You can tell Bigfoot that Gav wants to play in a decent band,' Fitch said, putting his arm around Gav's shoulders and smiling that close-lipped smile of his. 'Tell him we've got the best drummer in Cleeston back where he belongs.'

The best drummer in Cleeston looked embarrassed. He wouldn't meet my eyes.

'We've got our first gig next month,' Fitch continued, obviously gloating. 'You can come free if you want. You might learn something.' He turned to Gav. 'Come on, we've got some rehearsing to do.'

'G-give us a minute,' Gav said. 'I'll be there in a minute.'

Fitch shrugged, and went to walk away. Then he changed his mind and came right up to me, pushing his face in mine. 'Think yourself lucky, sap.' He shoved me, and I slipped, but didn't fall over. He laughed anyway as he walked over to his car.

'I'm s-s-sorry, Danny,' Gav said when he was out of earshot.

'Don't worry about it,' I told him. 'But do you really want to play for Fitch again?'

He shrugged. 'I failed m-my m-mocks.'

It was a strange reply, but I understood what he was saying. 'Oh.' I nodded. 'Right.'

'And, you know, at least w-we're playing g-g-gigs.'

'Yeah. I guess so.' I looked over at the white Escort. 'You know, Will reckons that it was Fitch who started the fire.'

Gav didn't answer.

'What do you think?' I asked.

'I don't know,' he said reluctantly. 'M-maybe.'

I shook my head. 'Are you sure you want to hang around with a guy like that?'

'He's got a b-b-band,' Gav said. Then: 'Come see us.'

'Shoot Cliff's not really my scene.'

'We're loads b-b-better,' he said. 'We're c-called DTM now.'

'DTM? What's that stand for?'

'Duh-Death to Manilow. It was F-Fitch's idea.'

I had to laugh. 'I don't doubt that for a minute,' I told him.

But things were awkward between us and I could tell he was itching to get back into the Escort with his band mates. 'Look,' I said, 'I hope it works out, good luck with the gig and everything.'

He nodded. 'Yeah. Thanks, Danny. Say hi to Will, yeah?' He turned and walked away.

'And say hiya to your dad from us,' I shouted.

He nodded again. Fitch revved the engine and Gav climbed into the back seat. I didn't blame him. I should have realised sooner exactly what he'd been talking about in my bathroom on New Year's Eve. He really was talented, his drumming was what he had to offer the world, and it was all he knew how to do well. He needed to be in a band. He needed to play.

I walked away myself then. I didn't bother looking for the Gibson in the music shop. I felt peculiarly hollow inside, but didn't fully understand why. And it was only when I got to Beth's house that I remembered I hadn't said thank you to him for saving me from a beating.

Forcing the Decision

Beth was wearing a black bra. She'd bought it especially because I'd told her how much I fancied girls who wore them. She giggled when she told me she had it on. I liked her giggle too; it was easily as sexy as the bra.

'I don't believe you,' I said.

She didn't understand. 'What do you mean?'

'I don't believe you're wearing a black bra,' I told her. I smirked cheekily at her. 'You'll have to prove it.'

She gave me an over-the-top look of disgust. 'No way.' She made a great show of crossing her arms over her chest. 'I don't care if you believe me or not. I know the truth.'

'Maybe I'll make you prove it.'

'In your dreams.'

I shrugged, then grabbed her and pushed her onto my bed. She squirmed and kicked and managed to wriggle out from underneath. I fought back, but she was bigger than me. She swung a long leg across my belly and crouched over me. She was wearing a short, brown skirt which rode up high around her thighs. She had me pinned down. Not that I cared, because I was looking at her thighs.

I was in love, no doubt about it. This girl was fantastic, wonderful, absolutely amazing. And she wanted to be with me. That was the most surprising part. Who'd have guessed it? Beth Simmons wanting to spend time with Danny Graham? Miracles did happen. It had been a shaky start admittedly, both thinking the other was only doing it to get at Will in some way, but we'd made a pact a few weeks ago not to mention his name. He obviously didn't want anything to do with us, so we'd decided not to have anything to do with him either.

'I suppose you think you're clever, don't you?'

She nodded. 'Yep.'

'And I suppose you think I'm trapped and can't get up?'

She leaned forward and bit my nose with her sharp teeth just to prove exactly how much in control she believed she was.

'But did you know I can see your knickers from here?'

She squealed in indignation, letting my arms go so she could make a grab for her skirt. So I suddenly sat bolt upright, tipping her backwards. Then *I* was on top, with *her* pinned down.

'Apologise,' I said. 'Tell me I'm great. Tell me I'm the king.'

She bucked and thrashed. 'Never. Never.'

I was writing a song about her. I hadn't told her yet because I wanted it to be a surprise. I hadn't even told her that I still played my guitar, and I always made sure it was hidden in my wardrobe whenever she came round to see me. Some of the time I was trying to teach myself new songs, but I still enjoyed playing the old Happy stuff too. I thought they sounded great and felt kind of proud at having had a hand in writing them. I'd come up with a brilliant new solo for 'Chasing Summer' the other night; it was just a pity I didn't have anyone to play it to. I'm sure Will would have liked it. I was thinking about Will a lot actually. And Happy. Not that I would admit it to Beth if she ever asked.

Beth and I rolled and fought with each other on my bed, twisting up the sheets, getting breathless and sweaty. She pinched my arms, I flicked her ears. It was so childish, and *so much fun.* We were yelping and giggling like little kids. I was trying to tickle her; she was trying to kick me off the bed and onto the floor. We were both squealing with laughter. We must have been making a lot of noise because we didn't hear my dad knocking at the door. He had to walk into my room before we even knew he was there.

I literally leaped off the bed, desperate to put some sort of respectable distance between Beth and me. And immediately excuses started springing to mind. Beth sat up just as quickly, straightening her clothes. She was blushing horrendously, making me feel even more guilty. We were only messing about, I wanted to say. We weren't doing anything. My dad hovered in the doorway, not knowing where to look. Definitely not at Beth; he tried to pretend she wasn't there and stared straight at me, deciding it was probably the safest thing to do. He was red in the face, but I couldn't tell if it was through anger or embarrassment. And I wasn't sure which would be worse.

'Er, Danny. Could I have a word, please?'

I nodded quickly. 'Yeah. Of course. No problem.' I tucked my shirt into my jeans, trying to tidy myself up, then realised I was probably making things look far worse than they actually were. What a nightmare. Getting caught by your dad! He stepped outside into the hallway. I looked back at Beth and she rolled her eyes, still pulling her rumpled T-shirt straight. I followed him out and closed the door behind me.

I thought the safest bet would be to jump in first, get the excuse in straight away. 'I know what you're going to say, Dad, but we weren't . . .'

He waved my words aside, not letting me finish. 'You were just being a bit noisy, that's all.'

'Honestly, Dad. We weren't doing anything. We were just messing around . . .'

He smiled at me.

I was a little taken aback. 'It wasn't as if anything was going on,' I said.

He started laughing. 'I'm not worried about what was going on,' he said. 'You're old enough to know right from wrong.'

'Pardon?'

'I just didn't want Beth to think I was spying on her. You'll have to apologise to her for me. I had to come in because you didn't hear me knocking.'

I was shocked. My father the liberal? Surely not.

'I came up to tell you that Will's here.'

'Will?'

He nodded. 'I wasn't checking up on you, no matter how much your mother wanted me to.' He lowered his voice. 'I didn't want to send him up because Beth was here,' he whispered, gesturing at my door.

I gave him a quizzical look. It seemed to be taking me a while to twig on today.

'I thought it might be awkward if he didn't know about you and Beth.'

I was amazed. My father was showing a side of himself I'd never seen before: liberalism *and* thoughtfulness. But I didn't have time to think about it right now, because Will was downstairs.

He was standing just inside the front door, still wearing his coat. He looked normal enough. He didn't look as though he was upset with himself, or embarrassed about the fact that he'd been acting weird over the past few months. He smiled at me as I came down the stairs, following my father, who went through into the living room, leaving us alone. He was wearing his black jeans which had faded to grey at the knees, and his long hair was held back in a loose ponytail. He needed a shave. He had his guitar with him, in the black leather carry-case Beth had bought him when we'd first got the band together.

'Hiya, Danny,' he said. 'You all right?'

I nodded slowly. 'Yeah. Fine. How're you?'

'Great,' he told me, smiling even harder, nodding himself. Then: 'Listen, I've got a couple of new songs I've written, and I wanted to know what you thought of them. I think they're definitely my best so far, but I really want you to hear them too.' He lifted up his guitar in its case. 'I thought I could play them for you. There's one where I could do with a bit of help in the chorus, and I thought we could maybe invite Ian and Gav round to see if they had any ideas.'

I didn't know what I thought. He was acting as though nothing had happened. I hadn't said more than two words to him since the night of the gig. And yet here he was, talking about us, and Happy, as if it had only been four days instead of four months.

'You want to get the band back together?' I asked, and a little, involuntary thrill of excitement ran through me.

He looked shocked. 'Back together?' He seemed genuinely surprised. 'Did we ever split up?'

'But where've you been?' I asked.

He kicked his shoes off and laughed at me. 'Nowhere. I just decided I was glad the gig was a failure. I mean, if we're honest with ourselves, it was probably for the best, wasn't it? Those songs we'd written weren't good enough; I knew we could do better all the time. So I've been writing better ones, for when we start gigging properly.' He grinned at me. 'Trust me,' he said. 'These new songs are the best ever.' He walked straight past me and started up the stairs. 'Have you got Gav's telephone number? I forgot to bring it with me.'

I turned quickly to follow him. A thought suddenly came

to mind that I could play the new 'Chasing Summer' solo for him, and the song I'd written about Beth . . .

Oh, God. Beth.

'Will, just a minute.'

He stopped halfway up.

I struggled with the words, but there was only one way I could say it. I felt as guilty as I had only a few minutes earlier when my dad had walked in and caught us messing about. Maybe worse. I felt like it was Will's turn to catch me red-handed this time.

'Beth's in my room,' I told him.

I watched the emotions flicker across his face, from confusion to anger. He fought to hold them in and came up with a forced detachment, a faked indifference. He stood on the stairs with his guitar in his hand, gripping the handles of the carry-case, and bullied his face into blanking over. He was silent for several seconds. He nodded his head as if making a decision, seemed to think about it for a couple of seconds more, then nodded again in confirmation.

'Right,' he said. 'Yeah. Sorry. I didn't realise. I didn't mean to disturb you.' He pushed past me again, back down the stairs.

'You don't have to go,' I said. 'I just wanted to warn you in case . . .' In case what? I thought. In case . . . In case . . . 'I didn't think you knew she was here,' I added, sounding lame.

He stood by the front door and put his shoes back on. 'No, I didn't,' he said. 'Don't worry about it. It's not a problem.'

'Don't you want to see her?'

He met my eyes, but he didn't answer me. He stared at me, as if waiting for me say something else. To apologise maybe? To say I couldn't wait for his back to be turned because I'd been planning on stealing his girlfriend all along?

'I'll give you a ring, yeah?' I said.

He dropped his eyes. 'Whatever.'

He walked out, closing the door behind him.

And I was left standing in the hall wondering just what the hell had happened exactly. I thought maybe I should chase him, but told myself not to. He'd wanted to get the band back together. He'd spent all this time writing new songs. Was he going to try and get in touch with Gav and Ian? I should go after him, I thought. But couldn't quite bring myself to do it, because deep down I knew I didn't want Beth to see him. I headed back upstairs to my room. It crossed my mind not to tell her he'd been. Maybe she'd want to go back to him.

When I walked in she was straightening her hair in the mirror on my wardrobe door, fiddling with her slide.

'Are you in trouble?' she asked.

'Not exactly.'

She looked at me. I shrugged.

'Will came round,' I said, still wondering whether telling her about it was the right thing to do.

She paused while it sank in. 'When? Just now?'

'Yeah. He wanted to get the band back together – he had his guitar with him and everything.'

The emotions flickered across Beth's face exactly as I'd seen them flick across Will's, and she fought with them until she looked cool enough.

'Why did he leave? Because you told him I was here?' When I nodded she made a half-laughing kind of noise. It made her sound sarcastic, but hurt.

'He was talking about phoning Gav and Ian,' I said. 'He's been spending his time writing songs.'

Beth turned back to the mirror. She started fiddling with her hair-slide again.

'It was a bit of a shock,' I told her. 'He was acting as if nothing had happened. As if the band hadn't split up.'

'And has it?' Beth asked, her back to me. 'Have you split up, or were you just waiting for him to call you all back into line again?'

I wasn't sure what she meant.

'He obviously wants you in his band,' she said. 'But it's also obvious he doesn't want me around any more. Maybe you ought to choose between us,' she told me. 'He did.'

I didn't know what to say to that. I'd been frightened she'd leave me now that Will was out of his mood and back on the scene again, but it felt like the opposite was true; she was scared I'd leave her.

But I knew what she said was right. I knew I had to make a decision now. What meant more to me? A girlfriend, or a band? Maybe it was unfair of her to push me into choosing like this, but then again maybe I wasn't being particularly fair with her either. I'd still been holding out hopes for the band, hadn't I? Deep down. I had kept on telling myself the opposite was true, but . . .

The evening turned awkward between us. We both became moody and quiet. Beth left soon afterwards, making me feel rotten, but there was nothing I could do about it. I saw her off at the door, it was only a brief kiss, then I headed back upstairs and took my guitar out from its hiding place in my wardrobe. I played a few of the old songs. I played the song I'd been writing for Beth. I had the feeling that it should be an easy choice really, it was just that I was too stupid to see. I couldn't remember ever feeling quite as miserable as this before. I snapped one of the strings and lay back on my bed staring up at the ceiling.

I decided I'd talk to Will tomorrow. I'd go to see him at the comp and tell him exactly how I felt. But of course I never did, because by that time he'd already disappeared.

THE ADVERT

Everything went crazy for a week. Both Beth and I suddenly became the centre of attention with a whole host of questions about Will aimed at us. The first I knew about what had happened was when his grandma came round to ask if I had any idea where he was. Then the next day the police showed up at the comp and I was taken to a quiet room where they asked me a hundred and one questions about him. And the day after that Mr Holloway dragged me into his office to lecture me about the dangers of misguided loyalty. My parents insisted I stop being childish and put everybody's mind at ease, but I didn't have a single thing to tell them. I had as much of an idea about where he'd gone as they did. And Beth was the same. He hadn't dropped a hint, or left a note, or phoned us. He had quite literally disappeared off the face of the earth.

I began to get the feeling I was the one to blame. It certainly seemed as though I was the one in trouble. I lay awake in bed at night and wondered where on earth he could be. I wondered if he was looking for his father. Maybe he'd gone to become famous – he'd taken his guitar with him, after all. I wondered how I'd feel if he made it, if the next time I saw him was on *Top of the Pops*?

It would have been easy to assume that everything would have fallen into place between Beth and me without Will's shadow hanging over us, but it didn't seem to work out that way. We got caught up in what was happening; he seemed to come between us more now that he wasn't around. My parents didn't seem to want to let me out of their sight in case I was going to make a crafty phone call, or tap out a Morse code message, or something. I know it sounds melodramatic, but it's true. So I didn't get to talk to her about my feelings, about my decision. The problem was, the longer I went without seeing her, the more difficult it became. Neither of us really knew how the other felt; we were both frightened of getting hurt. And soon we both started avoiding each other at the comp. It seemed easier that way.

Luckily the madness only lasted a couple of weeks. Or at least the Will madness only lasted a couple of weeks. By the end of the month our family had the pregnant Deborah madness to worry about. It had taken her this long to pluck up the courage to talk to our mum about it, but only after a lot of insisting from Ian. And exactly as I'd predicted, my mother was the maddest of all. Her anger eclipsed the whole house. It was the first time in my life I'd ever felt sorry for my sister.

I kept out of the way as best I could. Ian came round most nights to try and help sort things out. He looked pale and haggard nowadays, like a real parent, and I wondered if he regretted being so insistent with my sister. I offered him quick, sympathetic smiles when I saw him, but stayed upstairs out of the way most of the time. What else could I do with the world falling apart around me? He and Debs would spend the night arguing with my mum and dad across the kitchen table.

It was on one of these nights that Gavin phoned.

'Oh, hiya, Gav,' I said. 'How're you doing?' I couldn't help letting the surprise in my voice leak out. This was the first time I'd spoken to him since he'd stopped Fitch from giving me a beating outside the music shop. 'Everything okay?'

'Sort of,' he said. 'Listen, c-c-can you talk?'

I looked down the hall and into the kitchen. Deborah was waving her hands around, her voice raised in protest, and my mum was yelling twice as loud.

'Not really,' I said.

'Can we meet?'

This surprised me again. 'Are you sure everything's all right?' I asked, beginning to worry.

'I'll meet you at your flu-flower sh-h-hop. I'll w-w-wait for you.'

'What's going on, Gav? You sound a bit freaked out.'

There was a pause. Then he said, 'I know where Will is.'

Was he serious?

'Yuh-you'll come quick, yeah?'

'Yeah,' I said, my mind racing. 'Yeah. Of course. I'll be as quick as I can.'

I needed transport. I went to the kitchen and timidly stuck my head inside the door, ready to pull it back like a turtle if it looked like there was any danger of me getting it bitten off. The four of them sat around the table, my parents on one side, my sister and Ian on the other. It looked as though it had at least started out diplomatically. I apologised for disturbing them and asked my dad if I could borrow the van.

'It's locked up in the garage,' he said sharply. 'What do you want it for?'

'Gav just phoned. I wanted to go and see him.'

Ian stood up quickly before my dad had chance to say anything else. 'I'll give you a lift,' he said. 'It'll save any hassle.' Both my mum and my sister went to complain, but he was already putting his shoes on and fumbling in his pocket for his keys. 'I won't be long,' he shouted from the hall.

I followed just as quickly, not wanting either of us to be called back.

'What's this all about then?' he asked as we climbed into his car. 'I didn't think Gav kept in touch any more.'

'He doesn't usually,' I admitted. 'But he says he knows where Will is.'

It was Ian's turn to look surprised. 'Straight up?'

I nodded. 'So he says.'

'I'm glad I came then,' Ian said, and started the car.

We drove along the dark streets towards the shop.

'How're my mum and dad treating you?' I asked. 'Now they know?'

'Your old man's not too bad,' he said. 'He's a nice bloke, he just wants the best for us.'

I nodded, although I maybe wouldn't have believed it up until a few weeks ago.

'And I guess your mum doesn't hate me as much as I thought she would,' Ian continued with a sigh. 'But there's not much anybody can do about the situation, is there? I think both of them understand that I love Debs, and that I want to do the best by her. That's the important thing.'

'Do you think you'll be happy getting married and that?'

'What do you mean?'

'Well, you know? You're only twenty-one.'

'Do you think I'm too young?'

I shrugged. 'I don't know. I suppose it's because I'm thinking about Will. Settling down seems to be the last thing on his mind.'

Ian smiled. 'You can say that again.'

I sighed. 'It's weird, isn't it?'

'What is?'

'Well, how the four of us have split up now,' I said. 'And everyone's going in different directions. It makes you wonder who's right and who's wrong.'

Ian laughed loudly. 'Don't ask me. I haven't got the foggiest.'

Gav was waiting for us when we arrived. He had a copy of last week's edition of the *NME* music paper under his arm. He seemed pleased that Ian had come as well and I realised that they hadn't actually seen each other since New Year's Eve. And I somehow doubted Gav would remember much of that. But it felt good that the friendship still held outside the band.

I opened the back door, reached inside for the light switch. Gav looked as though he might burst if he didn't tell someone his news soon. He rushed through into the little back room.

'Has Will been in touch?' I asked. But he shook his head. 'So how do you know where he is?'

'It's in here,' he said, waving his music paper.

'Will's in the *NME*?' Ian asked, incredulous. 'Are you serious?'

My heart jumped. For a fleeting moment I thought he'd made it. I thought he really had moved down to London and been snapped up by some record company or other.

Gav went straight over to the table and opened the paper out on top of all the cellophane and ribbon. He opened it near the back and started searching through the classifieds. Ian and I stood looking over his shoulders, one on either side.

'There,' Gav said. He jabbed his finger at an advert in the 'Musicians Wanted' section, then turned to watch our reactions.

I peered at the tiny print. It read: 'Are you Happy? I am. Drummer and bassist required.' And then a London telephone number.

Ian and I looked at it for a long time. I read it two or three times. I didn't know what to say. Could that really be Will? I turned to look at Ian, and he shrugged, pushing his glasses up his nose. Only Gav seemed convinced.

'It's guh-got to be,' he said. 'He's getting another b-b-band together.'

'Would he really use the same name, though?' Ian asked.

'Probably,' I said. 'He thought it was the perfect name for a band playing his music. He was always saying that. Don't you remember?'

Gav was adamant. 'It's Wuh-Will!' he told us. 'It h-has to be.'

'It's a London number,' I admitted. 'Everybody reckons that's where he would've gone.'

Ian nodded. 'True. His dad's got a flat there, hasn't he? Somewhere called Stepney, I think.'

'How did you know that?'

Ian shrugged. 'I asked him,' he said.

I was quite taken aback. Will had never told me. 'What else did you ask him about?'

'All sorts. I was curious about his dad, that was all.' He shrugged again. 'He told me he's a musician, plays session guitar for quite a few different people. Some famous ones too. That's why he's never around, he's always touring or recording with some band or other.'

'You what?' I was stunned. 'He never told me any of this. He never talked to me about his dad being a guitarist or any-thing.'

'Well, did you ask him?'

I didn't know what to say. I had to shake my head. But it seemed impossible that after all these years of knowing Will, I was only just finding out. I was his oldest friend. I wanted to feel betrayed, I wanted to feel cheated. But of course, I had never asked, had I? I'd never wanted to know anything about his father. Why would I want to know about the man who always brought Will presents? Expensive presents, presents which made me jealous. I was ashamed now of how petty minded I'd been, and remembered how I'd acted when Will had first started seeing Beth, and how I'd wanted a new guitar just because Will had been given one slightly better than mine.

Yes, it seemed impossible, but I really was the kind of person who'd never want to ask his oldest friend about his father. And to be honest, I couldn't blame him for not telling me. If he had, I would have probably never forgiven him.

But it was like a huge jigsaw piece had fallen into place, and the thunk inside my head was almost deafening.

'No wonder he wants to be in a band so bad,' I said. 'No wonder he was getting so worked up about it all the time.'

I felt so stupid because I'd never taken the time to ask. I shook my head again. What kind of a friend was I?

'Don't tell me,' I said. 'His dad used to do session work for Elton John, right?' Ian nodded. 'Well, at least that explains those CDs.'

Gav looked at me, confused. Ian got the joke at least and raised a small smile. But it really didn't make me feel any better about myself.

I read the advert one more time.

'That's Will,' I said. 'I know it now. That's him. Definitely.'

'But what do we do about it?' Gav asked.

'There's not much we can do, is there?' Ian said. 'Unless you want to move to London with him.'

'He's trying to be like his dad,' I said. 'He's trying to copy him.'

'We could ring him and see if he's okay.'

I nodded, but I wasn't really listening. I was wondering whether or not I had the guts. Did I dare?

Yes. Yes I did. I read the advert again, then ripped it out of the paper. I folded it neatly and put it in my back pocket.

Ian shook his head. 'You're not serious?' he said. 'You can't go to London.'

I shrugged. 'I owe him an apology.' I was beginning to think that it was me who had deserted Will. So I had to find him. I knew it was going to cause problems, but I had to.

Just . . . had to.

'Your mum's going to kill you,' Ian told me.

THE GIFT

But if I was going to try to sort things out with Will, then I reckoned I had to get myself sorted too, which meant talking to Beth. Her parents didn't like the idea of me being in her bedroom, so whenever we were together at her house we had to sit drinking coffee in the dining room. I supposed it was because her dad was a teacher, and over the years he'd simply got to know all too well what young lads could be like, what kind of thoughts usually filled their heads. We sat next to each other, resting our elbows on the table, but our chairs were still slightly apart. They were set at angles so we didn't have to look at each other if we didn't want to. I had a plastic carrier bag at my feet.

I'd rehearsed a special speech, especially. But I'd forgotten most of it now. The room was somehow imposing; I'd never liked it. The pictures of landscapes and wildlife, the tall cabinet with the posh china plates, the big polished table and the hard, upright chairs simply didn't fit with my impressions of Beth. The room was too dull, too old-fashioned. And it felt much too cold for what I wanted to say.

'I thought we needed to talk.'

Beth nodded. She was wearing jeans and a baggy T-shirt. She'd been embarrassed when I'd first turned up out of the blue and had wanted to get changed, but I hadn't let her. I needed to talk to her straight away, before I lost my nerve. She sat looking at her coffee cup, not at me.

'I just wanted to get things sorted.'

She nodded again. She wasn't going to make this any easier for me. I could have laughed in a dark kind of way; it summed her up perfectly. She was going to make me work, even at this.

'I wish you'd look at me.'

She raised her eyes to mine, but still didn't speak.

'I wish you'd talk to me.'

She sighed. 'One left,' she told me. 'You only get three, don't forget.'

I shook my head in despair. She simply wouldn't give me an inch. 'Come on, Beth . . .'

'What do you want me to say?'

'I don't know. Anything. Tell me what you're thinking?'

She shrugged. 'I'm thinking that you care more for Happy than you do for me, that I've been through all this before. And that if I ever have another boyfriend he's going to be tone deaf, he's going to hate music, and hopefully he won't have any hands so he wouldn't be able to pick up a guitar even if he wanted to.'

I did laugh then. 'Oh, is that all.'

'I don't see what's so funny.' She looked miserable. I ached to hold her, but I was frightened she wouldn't let me. 'I don't even know why you bothered coming round,' she said.

'Because I wanted to see you.'

She scoffed. I knew what she was doing. She was trying to keep me away, hold me at arm's length. She was waiting for me to tell her it was over between us, and wanted to keep a safe distance in an attempt to soften the blow.

'I know where Will is,' I told her.

I saw the look on her face. She tried to hide it, but I saw the surprise, and then the concern.

'I'm going to go see him,' I continued. 'He's in London; I've got a telephone number.'

'What are you doing that for?' she asked quietly.

'I guess I just feel bad about the way everything's turned out.'

'You mean because you stole his girlfriend?' she said with a nasty edge to her voice.

'No. Not at all.' I shrugged. 'You'd already decided it was over by the time I came along.'

'So why're you feeling so guilty?'

'I don't think I'm feeling guilty. Just a bit stupid. We've known each other for ages, and even if we were pretty horrible to each other sometimes, we were always friends. That's worth something, isn't it?'

Beth didn't answer. She was staring at her hands underneath the table. 'You didn't have to come round and tell me all of this,' she said. 'It's got nothing to do with me any more.'

'I wanted to sort things out with you as well.'

'I think it's pretty obvious what you've decided, isn't it?' She looked up at me. I'd never seen her look so unhappy before. She was waiting for me to push her aside. But that wasn't what I wanted to do.

The problem was that I had somehow become trapped by the band, because it had given me the chance to dream. When I'd met the others to rehearse, when I'd helped write songs, I'd left my normal life behind and felt part of something much more exciting. And the more involved in the band I'd become, the more dreary and boring everything else had seemed. I'd believed that if I gave the band up, I would have had to return to the old life which I'd already condemned, already deemed unworthy. What I'd forgotten, of course, was that my old life hadn't included Beth.

I knew I had to somehow prove this to her, however. I had to give her some sort of sign that I wanted to be with her more than anything else in the whole, big, wide world.

'I've brought you a present,' I said. I picked up the plastic carrier bag and put it down on the table in front of her. It clunked against the wood.

She looked at me suspiciously. 'What is it?' she asked.

'Open it and see.'

She still hesitated, but I could see how tempted she was. I shrugged at her, as if it didn't matter to me one way or the other, as if she could do exactly what she pleased. But I was as nervous as hell really.

'It won't bite,' I told her.

She pulled the bag a little closer to her, and peeked inside.

I felt my heart swell up in my chest. Almost instantly her mouth twitched at the corners, betraying the beginnings of a smile.

'Is this what I think it is?' she asked.

I nodded. The cold room was suddenly very warm, and I felt my cheeks go red as my face burned up.

'You're always telling me how much you like flowers,' I said. 'You haven't stopped going on about them since you found out my mum and dad owned a florist's.'

She couldn't hide her smile now. She reached inside the bag and pulled the sunflower free. Admittedly it looked as though it needed some attention; its massive yellow petals were slightly crumpled, but the little purple pot was as bright and shiny as it had ever been.

'I want you to have it,' I told her, 'because you make me happy.'

She tried to fight with her smile, to bring it down to a reasonable size. 'You soft sod,' she said.

I grinned at her. At last I felt as though I was doing something right. Now all I had to do was find Will; wherever he was, whatever he was doing.

THE FUNERAL

The church was fairly well hidden among the narrow side streets of Stepney, but I hadn't been the only one who had managed to find it. A long line of black cars was parked outside, their drivers leaning up against the bonnets, chatting, smoking. A group of kids was hanging around to see what all the fuss was about. It was the Easter holidays, the sun was out and they were all in shorts and T-shirts. I hesitated on the opposite side of the street. I still had my rucksack slung over my shoulder, my jeans and jumper were blue, not black, and I hadn't shaved for three days. I didn't feel particularly well dressed for a funeral.

There were two men working their way along the line of funeral cars talking to the drivers. I guessed they were journalists; I'd expected there to be more. When I'd plucked up the courage to cross the road one of them came over to me and started in with a hundred questions about how well I'd known the deceased, and just who on earth I was. I disappointed him by shrugging and staying quiet. I had nothing worthwhile to tell him.

I hadn't been inside a church since Will and I had been in the scouts, and to tell the truth, Church Parade had been one of the reasons I'd left. You don't think you need a church when you're younger; they only seem to become useful when you get older.

When I stepped inside the air suddenly became cooler. A

tall woman dressed all in black offered me a sympathetic smile and a sheet of paper. She didn't speak to me, simply gestured for me to carry on into the main body of the church. I glanced quickly at the paper she'd handed me as I walked through. There were no hymns printed on it; instead we'd all be singing Ben E. King's 'Stand By Me', 'Let It Be' by the Beatles, and a song I'd never heard of before called 'Waiting for You'.

There was a low chatter in the church, an almost secretive murmur which echoed softly around the walls. A few people turned briefly at the sound of my footsteps, but didn't recognise me, so dropped their gaze again. I chose a pew as close to the back as I could. There was a casket set on a low table at the front near the altar. Everybody was trying not to look, but like mine their eyes kept being drawn back to it. It was a deep, dark oak colour; the brass handles shone. A single wreath was propped against it.

I was beginning to feel horribly out of place, beginning to doubt my reasons for coming. This is wrong, I kept telling myself, I shouldn't be here. I hadn't exactly been invited. I was ready to leave, I felt almost claustrophobic. Then Will's grandma and grandad appeared behind me and walked quickly down to the front of the church, their footsteps echoing. The old lady held a handkerchief to her face, weeping quietly. The old man held her arm.

I'd arrived in London on Tuesday night and the first thing I'd done was phone the number in the advert, but no one had answered. I'd mooched around the streets, feeling let down and deflated. I'd imagined this great reunion with hugs and slaps on the back; it hadn't even crossed my mind he'd be out. I'd considered going into Stepney on the underground, where Ian had said Will's father had a flat, but I knew that all I'd be doing was wandering around the streets in the hope I'd suddenly turn a corner and see Will standing there. And I knew it was a ridiculous hope. So I'd hung around in the centre of London, trying to get excited by the shops, but I'd stopped at every telephone kiosk along the way to try the number again and again. I'd wasted most of Tuesday like that. I'd realised I should have done what Beth had suggested and let him know I was coming, but I didn't think he'd welcome me unless I kind of forced myself on him.

Beth had been right at the front of the queue to talk me out of doing this; she seemed to firmly believe in letting sleeping dogs lie. She'd said that if Will wanted to see me he would have been in touch himself, which I fully agreed with. But I wasn't just doing this for Will, I was doing it for myself as well.

By Tuesday evening I had become so frustrated I thought I might burst. I'd called my mother, just to let her know that I was okay and there was no need to worry, but it had been a huge mistake. It had cost me a fiver in change just to calm her down. I'd left Ian in charge of breaking the news to her gently, but it was obvious he hadn't succeeded. She'd ordered me home, using everything from my exams to my sister's pregnancy as emotional blackmail. For the first time in my life I'd disobeyed her. Or as Will would probably have said, I'd stood up to her. After which I hadn't any change left to try the number in the advert again, or any energy to carry on walking, so had retreated to find a cheap hotel and to save my optimism for Wednesday.

When the vicar appeared I realised it was too late for me to leave without making some sort of a scene. I stood up with the congregation and sang 'Stand By Me'. I wasn't particularly surprised to discover it wasn't the church organ which accompanied us, but a single acoustic guitar which played from a balcony above our heads. The notes were clear and precise, ringing slightly with the echo. I knew instinctively that it was Will, playing the guitar at his father's funeral.

When the song finished we all sat back down and the vicar talked about Max Brown; the friend, the father, the musician. He had a long and impressive list of credits to his name, he'd played guitar for a lot of famous people, but had never quite hit the big time himself. Which was all part of his character, or so we were told. Not a front man, but a strong support.

I watched the mourners as the vicar spoke, and thought it was quite strange to see how little they apparently seemed to be mourning. The only tears I'd seen were from Will's grandparents. We stood up again and sang 'Let It Be', once more backed by the single acoustic guitar from above us.

I'd had a brainwave on Wednesday morning and had hurried to get out of the hotel, not least because of the dirty sheets, noisy neighbours and freezing water. I'd rung the *NME* offices and had tried to get them to give me more details about the advert, pretending that I was a drummer and explaining how I couldn't get through on the printed number. But the man I'd spoken to simply wasn't interested. He said they printed the adverts in good faith and they really had nothing to do with him. I'd begged for any further scrap of information he might have, but he'd been immovable and unsympathetic. And once again I'd been up against a brick wall and an unanswered phone.

This time I had caught the underground to Stepney, and this time I had wandered around, getting myself lost and over hopeful. By the end of the day I'd been exhausted both physically and mentally, and I certainly hadn't been relishing the prospect of spending another night in that stinking hotel, the only one I could afford. But that had been what it came down to.

I had, however, had one final idea, and at the time it had really felt like the last one I might ever have. I'd bought a copy of the *Melody Maker* to take back to the hotel with me. I'd been hoping that Will had placed his advert in both music papers, and at least a second ad would either confirm the telephone number, or prove a misprint in the *NME*. Unfortunately Will was being as elitist as ever, and had only gone to the most popular press.

Out of luck, out of ideas; I'd sat in my grubby hotel room flicking through the music paper I'd bought anyway, just to pass the time. Something had to happen tomorrow, I was thinking, because I was out of money too. Then at the bottom of a page, half-hidden and tucked away, I'd spotted a little notice about Max Brown's death and his funeral in Stepney.

'I'm sure Max Brown will be missed,' the vicar told us. 'As is anybody of great character. But I know his influence and his talent will live on for a new generation to appreciate, not just through the records he has helped to make, but also through his young son, Will.'

At the sound of his name Will appeared through the doors behind me and walked steadily down to the front of the church. He didn't notice me. He stood beside his father's casket. The acoustic guitar was slung over his shoulder. I was surprised to see how *normal* he looked. I don't know why, but just like when he'd come round to my house that last time, I expected him to have changed.

'We'll close the service with a final word from Max's son.

This is the last song on your sheet, and it is one which Will himself wrote for his father.'

The congregation got to its feet again. But no one sang a single note. Will and his extraordinary voice filled the church for us.

He sang: 'Still down, still blue, too old to be sniffing glue . . .'

I waited until the very last minute before I approached Will at the end of the service. He was standing with his grandparents, shaking hands with the line of mourners as they left the church. I didn't think he recognised me at first, or maybe I was the very last person he expected to see. It wasn't until his grandmother said my name with obvious astonishment that he clicked on to who I was. I had no idea how he was going to react to seeing me, and I still hung back a little. But his grandparents bundled me up, asking me what on earth I was doing here, and did my mother know? Will acknowledged me with a short nod, then headed back into the nave.

When I'd satisfied his grandparents that I was fit and healthy, if a little tired, I got the chance to follow him. He was standing by the casket. He turned at the sound of my footsteps.

'How're you doing?' I asked quietly, not liking the way the echo of the small church seemed to amplify my voice.

'Good,' he said. 'You?'

I said, 'Been better. You're hard to track down. Don't you ever answer the phone?'

'I've been busy with this,' he told me. Then, 'How'd you find me?'

'Gav saw your advert in the *NME*, which brought me down to London. Then I saw the little piece about your dad dying in the *Melody Maker*. I'm sorry, by the way.'

He nodded. 'Heart attack,' he told me. 'I was just getting to know him.' He ran his fingers along the coffin's lid.

'Are you burying him privately?' I asked.

'We're cremating him tomorrow, just my grandparents and me. Today was something I organised.'

I wasn't sure what he meant.

'The people here, I invited them all,' he explained. 'Record company bosses, A and R men, that kind of thing. I think it turned out all right in the end. A couple of them said they really liked the song, and gave me their cards to get in touch.'

I didn't know what to say. He'd set up an extra funeral service for his father just so he could get his foot in the doors of record companies. I was amazed. 'What do your grandma and grandad think?'

'I told them that these people had been in touch with me, wanting to pay their last respects.'

'Jesus, Will . . .' I started, but stopped not only because of the look on his face, but also because I suddenly remembered where I was. I lowered my voice. 'Don't you think that's a bit, well . . . You know?'

'A bit what?' he asked indignantly. 'Look, Danny, I came down to London to become a musician, and that's what I'm going to do, okay? My father told me it's a cut-throat business, and to do whatever I could to get to the top.'

'But . . .'

'There're no buts about it,' he told me. 'What's up, don't you think I can do it? I came down here to get away from people who . . .'

'Will, please. I didn't come here to give you grief.' I looked at him imploringly. 'I really didn't.'

He walked over to a pew and sat down. 'So what did you come here for?'

I moved across and sat next to him. 'To make sure you're

all right . . .' He went to scoff, but I wouldn't let him. 'To apologise,' I said. 'To be friends again. To be able to say goodbye and good luck this time.'

His frown lifted slightly. He took a deep breath. 'How's Beth?'

'Worried. Like Gav. Like Ian and my mum and everybody else I know. Why didn't your grandparents tell everybody you were okay?'

'They didn't know I was here at first, until I found out if it was all right to stay with my father. Then I just asked them not to say anything to anyone.' He leaned forward, resting his elbows on his knees and putting his face in his hands. 'Say hi to everyone for me.'

'No worries.'

'Especially Beth.'

I nodded.

'They're all okay, yeah?' he asked.

'Oh, yeah. Definitely.' I winced slighty. 'Well, sort of. Gav's back playing drums for Fitch, and Ian's about to be a dad.'

Will looked at me, shocked.

'Straight up,' I told him.

'What about you?' he asked.

'Me? Well, you know, I'll breeze through my exams, then go away and do English somewhere: Sheffield, Norwich maybe. I wouldn't mind trying to write a book.'

He nodded his approval. 'About time you did something worthwhile without me.'

We both laughed, our voices ringing loudly against the cold stone walls.

Will stood up again when the echoes finally died down. 'I'm going to make it,' he told me. 'One day.'

'I hope you do,' I said. 'I really want you to.' And as I said it, I realised I actually meant it. I suddenly got the urge to tell him I didn't care if his guitar was better or more expensive than mine. But instead I said, 'Listen, it's been good to see you, but I'd better go. I promised my mum I'd be home for tea.'

He grinned at me, and we stood looking at each other, trying to balance the years, weighing up everything that had happened.

'Look after yourself, yeah?' I said. I could feel tears pricking at my eyes. I turned away, feeling stupid, remembering all too clearly what had happened at the gig.

But Will wouldn't let me go. He hugged me, putting his massive arms around me. He held onto me for such a long time.

'I'm happy,' he told me. 'I hope you are too.'

Stop. Eject.

About the author

Keith was born and brought up in Grimsby and knew from an early age that he wanted to be a writer. When he got 0% in his accountancy exams he decided it was time for a career change and decided to make his writing dream a reality. His first book, *Creepers*, was published in 1996 when he was only twenty-four. The novel was highly acclaimed and shortlisted for the Guardian Fiction Award. His short novel, *The Runner*, won a Smarties Award. Keith is now a full-time writer. He lives in Edinburgh with his cockatiel, Baxter.